**She fought a shiver of delight.
Please don't touch me.
It just makes this harder.**

Instead of letting go, his fingers gripped her. "If after prayer and thought and time, we both believed we should marry, we wouldn't let my mom or anyone else stop us. Would we?"

She took a deep breath and looked him in the eye. "No. We wouldn't."

"Then what on Sunday changed your mind?" He tried to smile. "It wasn't my cooking, was it?"

She half laughed, half sobbed. "No, no, it was wonderful." *You were wonderful. You were everything I'd ever dreamed of....*

"Then what?"

She wanted to run away. She wanted to throw herself into those strong arms and never let him go.

"What, Lauren?"

RACHAEL PHILLIPS

(www.rachaelwrites.com), an award-winning fiction and nonfiction writer, lives only a county away from Peru, Indiana, home of the Circus City Festival and setting for *The Greatest Show on Earth*. She and husband, Steve, enjoyed researching the novel by attending this fabulous hometown event, where for more than forty years the children and teens of "Circus City" have performed juggling, trapeze, high-wire, unicycle, and acrobatic stunts, as well as many others, to amaze and delight their audiences.

The Greatest Show on Earth

Rachael Phillips

Blessings!
Rachael Phillips

Heartsong Presents

To Kim Peterson and Jaclyn Miller, dear friends and meticulous editors who helped me with this manuscript. Thanks to all the special children and adults of Peru, Indiana, "Circus City," who welcomed me to their practices, willingly answered my questions, and performed their marvelous shows, making this story possible.

A note from the Author:

I love to hear from my readers! You may correspond with me by writing:

Rachael Phillips
Author Relations
P.O. Box 9048
Buffalo, NY 14240-9048

ISBN-13: 978-0-373-48616-8

THE GREATEST SHOW ON EARTH

This edition issued by special arrangement with Barbour Publishing, Inc., 1810 Barbour Drive, Uhrichsville, Ohio, U.S.A.

Chapter 1

Did Texas stretch to infinity?

Lauren Pellegrino poured water in the radiator from a Spiderman water bottle; the clouds of vapor rising from her SUV's engine were finally subsiding. She wondered if other mothers—mothers who had driven a thousand miles alone—felt this way.

"Mom! Why won't the car go?" A pair of freckled noses pressed against the car windows. Two black moist ones snuffled fresh air from where she had opened the windows a crack.

Alone—if you don't count twin eight-year-old boys and two yellow Labrador retrievers the size of palominos. Lauren brushed back her stringy hair and prodded a confident smile into place. "It just needs a drink and a little rest, guys."

"Can we get out? Please, please, please?"

"Sorry. Interstates have too much traffic." Shivering in the chilly wind, she watched cars and semis zoom out of sight, into the gray-brown hills. She hated driving at high speeds. "We're almost to Kerrville. We'll camp there tonight."

The boys argued with her and then each other. Ethan jammed his elbow into Logan, who shoved him back. Twinkie and Dinky joined in the fray, rocking the car until Lauren thought it would flip onto its side. If only she had left the dogs back in California. But the boys already had endured too much heartbreak.

The radiator had cooled. The sibling battle had not. *I just can't get into that car, Lord.*

She almost found herself asking God to keep the steam rolling from the hood.

She counted to ten. Twenty. A hundred. The brawl inside her SUV escalated to *Friday Night SmackDown* proportions. *Get in the car, Lauren. Are you a mom or a mouse?*

"Just call me Minnie." She sounded whinier than the Labs during thunderstorms. Lauren shook herself. More delay would only prolong this exhausting day.

She marched back to the driver's side, opened the door, and slid behind the wheel.

"Boys, if you ever want to get out of this car again, you'd better stop *this instant.*"

The threat worked—or at least, the war faded to whispered aggression and furtive punches. She started the car and pulled back onto the interstate, praying for the Rapture.

Miracle number one: they all arrived at the Kerrville KOA camp alive. Miracle number two: Lauren set up the tent on her first try.

"Good job, Mom." Logan gave her Brent's brilliant smile.

"Thanks, hon." She tried to return the grin. In a hundred different ways, the twins reminded her of their dad. She hurried to find the Labs' leashes. "Let's take the dogs for a walk."

Who took whom? Twinkie and Dinky yanked her and the twins along as other campers gave them a wide berth. Beside every giant RV, a rabid-sounding Chihuahua or Yorkie challenged her dogs. Lauren barely dragged them back to their site then tied their leashes to the weathered picnic table.

"Dad would climb the highest hill." Ethan pointed at the surrounding rugged range, tinted brassy gold by the setting sun through purple clouds.

"Yes, he would." She kept her voice level as she held up a jug and gestured toward the nearby community faucet. "Please go fill this. Stay out of the road. Don't talk to strangers. And stay dry. I don't want to do extra laundry unless I have to."

During the brief, blessed semiquiet, Lauren gulped the crisp air and tried to appreciate the beauty of the place. But the hills only reminded her Brent had climbed one mountain too many.

She flipped open the cooler. Still plenty of hot dogs. Enough that she could make their evening seem like a fun outing instead of a financial necessity.

Twinkie wagged her enormous golden body, shaped like her cakey namesake. The dogs jerked at their leashes, begging with liquid brown eyes.

"You really have been good puppies." Lauren filled old plastic dishes with dog food and water, sneaking them half a hot dog apiece.

She dumped charcoal into a little hibachi. The boys dashed up. "Are we gonna roast marshmallows?"

"After supper." She nodded then winced. Uh-oh. More purple clouds. The wind picked up, and the tent breathed like a living thing.

She shoved the unlit hibachi into the back of the SUV, grabbed bologna, bread, and raisins. She paused. Tent or car? Maybe they should settle in for the night. "Sorry, guys. Looks like it's going to rain. We'll roast marshmallows another night. Head for the tent. And bring the water.

"You, too." She untied the dogs, refusing to leave them in the rain. "Smell you for the next fifteen hundred miles? No way."

She didn't relish sharing close quarters with the Labs, but she couldn't shut them in the car, or they'd gnaw the seat covers or pee on their favorite spot—the driver's seat.

She unzipped the tent and herded her horde inside. Brent bought this large tent—cheap, but spacious enough for the whole family. He'd taken his pro-level tent on his final climb up Mount Hood....

"It's dark." Logan nuzzled her, and she handed him a flashlight.

"I'm starved!" Ethan tugged on her arm.

"Just a minute." The Labs trampled them. "Twinkie, Dinky, *lie down.*"

The Labs plopped side by side. Lauren vowed to record this exact voice, this mysterious tone that worked such magic on kids and dogs.

She slapped sandwiches together for the twins then "Frisbeed" bologna slices to the Labs, who caught them neatly and gobbled them. The dogs were a pain, but they provided security. If anyone dared approach the tent without an invitation, he'd find himself legless.

Splat. Splat-splat-splat.

"We're having a picnic, anyway!" She pasted on her best mommy smile.

As Ethan and Logan munched, raindrops danced on the faded canvas roof like little goblins. Thank the Lord, no thunder, and the wind remained at bearable levels. Lauren nibbled raisins, almost too tired to eat, checking for telltale tent leaks with her flashlight. She had spent hours coating the seams with waterproofing before they left Los Angeles. Would the tent hold up? As they finished eating, she drew a sigh of relief. So far, so good.

She gave thanks she'd chosen the warmer, southern route to the Midwest, making their inexpensive campouts possible. They couldn't afford hotels—even if she found ones that would accept the Labs. Lauren threw a glance toward them.

Both wagged at her, slapping their tails against the tent wall. Fat chance.

Still, February nights could grow cold in central Texas. She fingered the thick linings of the boys' new sleeping bags that would keep them toasty even if temperatures dropped. "No need to change clothes, guys. We'll shower tomorrow."

No objections from the twins. Not surprising. Lauren snuggled them deep into the comfy bags. Twinkie lay beside Ethan's bed, just as she had at home, and Dinky cuddled close to Logan. Lauren prayed with them. At the boys' request, she blessed Grandmamma—her mother-in-law—though she'd rather not.

"Bless Uncle Horton, too." Ethan already had adopted Lauren's uncle, the kind elderly man who had invited them to stay with him in Indiana.

She kissed them and then covered the flashlight with a towel as a makeshift night-light.

Soon Lauren heard nothing but breathing. No wheezing. Logan's asthma hadn't caused any difficulty—so far. She prayed his good health would continue and that breathing problems would not force her to separate him from Dinky at night.

The boys slept. The dogs slept. Lauren wiggled into her own sleeping bag, hoping the rain would let up. That they would arrive in Indiana before the SUV required last rites.

Perhaps the quiet was not such a good thing. Too much opportunity to think.

If only Brent were here. More than a year after his death, the words still echoed inside her, as if she were made of tin, as hollow as *The Wizard of Oz* character. But unlike him, she had a heart, and her heart missed Brent—though he probably would be no help with the car or anything else. As a Hollywood stuntman, Brent did miracles. As a husband and father…not so much.

She slid her sleeve across her wet eyes. Worry dug at her

nearly empty stomach. If the car collapsed completely, she couldn't call Uncle Hort. He was too old to make a long trip. Besides, he already had gone the second and third mile in inviting them to live with him. Brent's sister, Liz, an artist from Portland, made it clear after his funeral that children would not fit into her apartment or her life.

That left Brent's mom, Marian. She and her "gentleman friend," as she called Preston—though Lauren guessed he was no gentleman—would come to Lauren's rescue.

She sat up. She did not want her boys growing up in their house. *Lord God, we cannot go back there.*

Jesus knew. If she hadn't believed in Him, she never would have attempted this insane trip. Lauren pictured His arms around her. *We'll soon be halfway to Indiana.*

Finally she nestled into the sleeping bag, but not too deeply, because she didn't like anything covering her head.

Plink. Pause. *Plink.*

A cold drip of water hit her forehead. *Plinkety-plink.*

It was going to be a long night.

"Mom, we just gotta stop," Logan whined.

Lauren gripped the steering wheel, not budging her gaze from the semitrailer roaring past. Flocks of snowflakes hit the windshield like insects. "We stopped half an hour ago." Maybe the mad in her voice would keep the quaver out.

But she should be patient. Moms were *patient.* "We'll eat after Indianapolis. Then, last stop, Uncle Horton's in Peru!" *If I'm not arrested on double charges of child and dog abuse before then.*

"But it's snowing now. Let's build a snowman." Ethan unclicked his seat belt and plastered himself against the car window, shoving Twinkie aside. She jumped into the front seat and climbed into Lauren's lap.

"Twinkie! Ethan!"

Her grinning son knew she couldn't reach him. She elbowed Twinkie, who licked her face before moving to the passenger side. A passing driver leaned on his horn.

Sitting behind Lauren, Logan didn't attempt to unclick. But he wailed, "What if the snow melts?" Dinky whined then, joined in his human's misery with a sympathetic *"Ah-ooooo."*

"All right, *all right*." Lauren no longer cared about consistency in parenting. She just wanted them to survive the interstate. "There's a rest area two miles ahead. We'll stop there."

"Yay!" Logan switched moods. Ethan, still beltless, bounced on the seat. Lauren shoved Twinkie away again as she exited. She couldn't wait to dump this crowd into the snow. She'd have to retain ownership of the boys, but if the dogs ran away, so much the better.

The moment she braked to a stop, her passengers exploded out of the SUV into the soft gray-and-white winter landscape. Lauren dashed after the boys, frantically waving parkas she'd purchased from the Salvation Army. She grabbed leashes as Twinkie and Dinky sprinted from bony tree to tree—knowing she was, as usual, outnumbered four to one.

"Mom, look! We're angels!"

Choking back a strong denial, Lauren looked. One stocky little body, one thin one. Arms and legs flailing in the pale snow. Damp blond curls escaping dark hoods. Two pairs of sparkly blue eyes, and two grins stretched wide as heaven.

"You be an angel, too, Mom!"

Lord, You know I'm not. Nevertheless, Lauren flopped onto her back and spread her arms. The snowflakes had grown and softened, fluttering into her face like winter butterflies. The sky stretched over her, a fuzzy, silver-gray blanket. Brent died in a snowstorm. But this nearly empty rest area felt like a place of prayer.

Until two warm doggy tongues slathered her face.

"Stop it." She laughed, grabbing them. "Boys, help me get leashes on these two."

After capturing the dogs, she and the boys built their snowman. Lauren found old walnuts and shriveled red berries on thorny bushes that gave him a face. She also surrendered her fifty-cent hat. Wearing it at a rakish angle, the boys' lopsided, cockeyed Frosty looked positively debonair.

After a bathroom break and watery hot chocolate from vending machines, the boys took the Labs on a final run. Sipping the last warm, awful-tasting drops, Lauren realized she'd been too crazy the past hundred miles to notice the land around her looked flat as a floor. Black lace of distant trees lined the horizon, but the mountains that surrounded her out West had slipped away. Even the rolling hills of Kentucky and southern Indiana had said their farewells.

"I lift up my eyes to the mountains—where does my help come from?"

The mountains had seemed protective, but they'd taken Brent away. The ache that never left welled up in her throat; maybe she wouldn't miss them as much as she thought.

"My help comes from the Lord, the Maker of heaven and earth."

"Is that what You're trying to teach me?"

The twins and Labs, roaring back, didn't give God much time to answer. But when they all dozed off in the car, she thanked God for His presence and His protection. As twilight and Indianapolis rush-hour traffic closed in from all sides, Lauren fixed her eyes ahead and hummed a praise song.

Not one more mile. Not even half a mile.

Lauren pulled between lollipop reflectors into an icy driveway. Her exhausted SUV slid sideways again. She pumped the brakes, and her car bucked then shuddered to a stop. The glow from the porch spotlighted her like a circus performer. A voice boomed across the now crunchy snow.

"Laurie-girl. Glad you made it in one piece. Nasty night out. Come right in and get warm."

Ethan and Logan didn't stir, but the Labs did. Lauren's

weary mind tried to remember: she *had* told Uncle Horton
about the dogs, hadn't she?

His silhouette opened the car door, and before she could say
"hello," Twinkie plunged over her and shot out like an escaped
prisoner. Dinky, barking at the top of his lungs, tried to follow. Ethan yelled, still half asleep, and Logan broke into tears.

Lauren had spent her last dollars for the boys' hamburgers.
She would need the remaining credit on her card for Logan's
medicine and emergencies. If Uncle Horton didn't welcome
the dogs, where would they go?

"So you did bring the boys' pets. I got lots of room for 'em
to run. Room for dogs and boys. But we'll do that tomorrow."
Strong, knotty hands helped her out of the front seat.

Lauren opened the back door and cuddled Logan, who
quieted. "This is Uncle Horton, hon. He's going to take us
inside where it's warm."

"Boy, am I glad to see you." Ethan threw his door open.
"I don't ever want to ride in this car again!"

Uncle Horton chuckled. "Can't say I blame you." He helped
the boy navigate the icy patches. "I'll whistle for your hounds."

A deafening note echoed in the frozen night air. The dogs
came running as if they'd heard it all their lives.

Lauren cleared her throat. *"Sit."* Was this the magic voice?
It was. They did.

"Let's all go inside and thaw out in front of the fire. I made
oatmeal cookies, just like the ones your Aunt Kate used to
bake." He swept them toward the door and held it open. The
dogs beat everyone inside.

Aunt Kate's cookies? Though Lauren supported a still-
sleepy Logan, she felt as if she'd shed two decades between
the car and the house.

The boys were eating vegetable soup for supper. *Vegetable* soup. Like a magician, Uncle Hort had bewitched them.
Lauren dipped her spoon into the steaming, brown crock-

ery bowl of homegrown potatoes, corn, carrots, tomatoes, and green beans. The twins turned up their noses at any canned soup that might contain a nutrient. But sitting at Uncle Hort's old, nicked kitchen table, they were devouring their supper almost as fast as they had wiped out his oatmeal cookie supply.

It was enough to restore her optimism.

Almost.

"Feeling better, Laurie?" Though grayer, Uncle Hort moved around the 1970s kitchen like a younger man. His dark brown eyes twinkled, bright and kind as ever.

"I should. I slept till ten."

"You took a nap, too." Logan sounded as if she'd done something illegal.

"Your mom needed it." Uncle Hort patted her shoulder. "She's a real hero, driving all that way by herself."

"She wasn't by herself." Ethan stuck his chin out. "She had us."

"You're right." Uncle Hort nodded solemnly. "Good thing, or she might really have been tuckered out."

"Absolutely." So nice to have another adult at supper. She'd felt alone long before Brent died, what with his adventuring at work and at play. She'd learned not to ask questions about either—

"You feeling up to a little outing this evening?"

Uncle Hort's voice held an eager note, covered with layers of politeness. The boys' ears perked up.

"What do you have in mind?" Lauren tried to sound interested.

"Peru's playing Warsaw tonight at the gym. I think we can beat them this year."

Basketball. Of course. How could she forget his passion for the game, third only to God and his family?

"We wanna go!" Two boys, one voice.

"I thought you'd be tired after playing in the snow all afternoon." If only she could receive an energy transfusion from her kids.

"We're not tired!"

She could see that.

"The game's at seven." Uncle Hort checked the black-and-orange striped schedule next to his prayer list, both posted by the wall phone. "I could take 'em there and let you rest."

It sounded *so* tempting to sleep another twelve hours. But her earlier dreams had attacked her like enemies. If Lauren stayed home alone, the questions—What are we doing here? What will we live on? What was I thinking?—would land on her like a thousand bloodthirsty mosquitoes.

"I—I'll go, too."

She was sorry the minute she said it.

Too late. The boys cheered, "Mom's going with us!"

"Yay, Tigers!" Uncle Hort pumped his fist.

"Yay, Tigers!" The boys leaped from their chairs and cheered.

Too much time to think? Not a problem now.

Orange and black. The gym's bleachers overflowed with the colors because, as Uncle Hort told them before tip-off, both teams were the Tigers.

"But we're the Bengal Tigers." He stuck his chin out—the same way Ethan did, Lauren realized.

All coherent conversation ended with a primeval roar as the teams took to the floor. The noise did not diminish for the next two hours, not even during halftime, when the two schools' bands dueled to see who could play the loudest. The boys loved it all. Noise was a language they understood.

She, on the other hand, comprehended very little. Uncle Hort shouted explanations, but she couldn't decipher his meaning.

The high school basketball games Lauren recalled didn't trigger this rocket-launch decibel range. The cheer blocks bellowed incessantly. Dozens of old ladies wearing team sweatshirts rose to shake little fists at the referees. Thankfully Lauren couldn't understand the comments of the row of men behind her—only the growls and howls of their protests. When the entire Peru crowd rose in outrage, she did, too. At this point, another fake restroom visit was in order.

"Ahhhhhhh!" She screamed as a frozen stream poured down her back.

A big hand rested on Lauren's shoulder then turned her around.

She couldn't hear what this enormous farmer guy was saying, but she read the abject apology in his surprising little-boy face. He gestured with the now-empty soda cup as she tried in vain to dab her favorite blue sweater with a tissue. In a deep voice, he continued his attempts to explain.

Okay, okay. Lauren summoned a forgiving smile. The horde sat down, and finally, he did, too. The cold, sticky liquid glued her sweater to her back and soaked into her jeans. Now she needed a real restroom break.

She turned back to her family. Uncle Hort and the boys hadn't even noticed her predicament. She reached past the twins and tapped him on the arm, but the scoreboard changed. Uncle Hort and the kids popped up. The bleachers rumbled and shook as the giant behind her leaped to his feet and let out an ecstatic roar.

At least, this time, his soft-drink cup was empty.

Chapter 2

It wasn't a barn this evening; it was a battlefield.

"Mom, I know where this is going." Kyle stopped working with the horses and crossed his arms.

"Whatever are you talking about?" Rose Hammond whisked down the first aisle between stacks of rabbit cages. She turned up the volume of the Conway Twitty country-music hits that kept her bunnies happy—or so she insisted.

Kyle gritted his teeth. Mom already had fed her fifty-four darling pets. She just didn't want to look him in the eye.

"You're pushing me into a blind date again." He tried not to raise his voice. "It's not going to work."

She clucked her tongue. "I am not pushing you into any-thing. I just said it would be nice if you went out to dinner with your dad and me after church Sunday."

"Just us?" He didn't have to ask where. His parents always went to the Circus City Grill.

"We invited the Sharps." She emerged from the other end of Rabbit City and crossed to the scarred old desk where they kept paperwork. Mom opened the yellowed Tupperware container resting there, turned, and gave him a sweet smile.

Even across the barn, he could smell them. Freshly baked snickerdoodles. His favorite. The cinnamony fragrance rolled over him like a delicious avalanche.

Mom, you are so not playing fair. Fighting the urge to grab one, he demanded, "This wouldn't have anything to do with the fact the Sharps' granddaughter from Fort Wayne is visiting this weekend, would it?"

"How—" His mom bit her lip then rummaged through the drawers—a ploy, if he ever saw one. Mom knew the location of every paper clip and feed pellet on this farm. She cleared her throat. "They have a granddaughter your age?"

"She's seven years younger. At least, that's what I heard you say on the phone when you thought I'd left for my church meeting."

Point for me. He might be thirty, but he still enjoyed backing Mom into a corner.

"All right." She banged a drawer shut, her blue eyes snapping. "All *right*! So I hoped you would make Jenna Sharp feel welcome, maybe show her around a little. I'm not asking you to marry her—"

"You aren't?" He'd been through this so many times, he abandoned the script he knew by heart. "Sure you haven't bought the ring yet, Mom? Rented the tuxes?"

Perhaps he overstepped this time. From the look on Mom's face, he might lose a finger if he tried to filch a cookie. Sighing, he opened the stall where his horse, Flourish, greeted him with a sympathetic whicker.

"What's this about renting tuxes?"

He couldn't see his father, but he heard the clump of his big shoes, one dragging a little. "You haven't found a girlfriend, have you?"

"And he never will. He'd rather talk to that horse than a girl." Mom's voice brightened a little. Kyle was outnumbered, so she resumed the assault. "I don't understand it. You dated lots of nice girls during high school and college. And Brittany—"

"Brittany is getting married, Mom. Please don't bring her up again." He'd moved on after their breakup more than a year ago, but Mom hadn't. Kyle grabbed a rake and began to muck out the stall.

"But surely there's someone—"

"I came home after college, right? I dated the women around here. I—and they—decided they weren't for me."

"Which is why you should at least meet Jenna."

Rats. Point for Mom.

"I fed the cattle." Dad sounded weak. Was his leg worse? His tone also implied there was plenty more to do.

"I'll finish the rest." *Both of you, please go watch* Wheel of Fortune. *Please.*

"It wouldn't hurt you to eat Sunday dinner with us." Dad crunched into a cookie.

Kyle also knew where this was going. Soon Dad would remind him how much he wanted to see the grandsons who would farm his land. They'd had Kyle later in life, and now they were pushing him to marry. How he wished he wasn't an only child.

"All right. All *right*." Kyle threw down the rake—realizing he'd just echoed his mother's earlier words. He shoved the stall door open and tried not to glare at them. "I'll join you, the Sharps, and their granddaughter on Sunday. But that doesn't mean I'll ask her out. So don't send out the wedding invitations yet."

Mom's infuriating smile returned. Dad helped himself to four more cookies before they headed for the door.

They'd won again.

He turned on his heel, grabbed the stall gate, and slammed it behind him so hard Flourish jumped. Why did he feel as if they had just grounded him? He picked up the rake and attacked the dirty straw again.

Ruby, a feisty chestnut mare, neighed at him from another stall.

"Don't *you* start in on me." Kyle made a face at her. "I'll clean your stall in a minute. What is it about you moms, anyway?"

He might have to listen to his mother nag, but he didn't have to listen to her music. At least, not now. Kyle strode to the ancient boom box and cut short Conway's loud lament about lost love. "Too bad, rabbits. Get used to peace and quiet, for a change."

He began to relax, whistling between his teeth. But he felt silly, too. Wasn't he a little old to slam doors like a teenager? One more you'd-make-a-cute-couple ploy by his folks shouldn't cause a major meltdown.

But it went deeper than that. "You'd think by now they'd catch on." He stopped working and petted Flourish's nose. "I told them I want God to guide every aspect of my life, especially something so important."

But Jesus never guaranteed his parents would understand the change in his heart and lifestyle. In fact the Bible said families would clash about those differences, even families who attended church every week.

He threw down fresh hay. "You and I both know I'd like to marry," he told God and Flourish. "But I don't want to pick some girl's name out of a hat then grab a preacher. I want her to be the one You have for me, Lord. I want us to marry on Your schedule."

He grinned. "Wouldn't mind if she had big brown eyes, too. And blond hair. Always liked the combination." A video of the woman at the Warsaw ball game played on his mind's screen. He knew everybody in Peru, but she, with her sun-kissed hair and doe eyes, must be a newcomer—maybe a friend or relative of Horton Hayworth, sitting near her. Were those little kids hers? She was probably married. He grimaced. Even if she was single, maybe it was best she remained a stranger. After that spilled-soda incident, she probably didn't want to know *his* name.

"So I'm not ready for the world's Top Ten Bachelors list." He pulled a carrot from his jacket pocket and held it out to Flourish, who grabbed it with big, velvety lips.

Horses were such great listeners. *Maybe Mom is right.* Lately he'd found it more peaceful to talk to them—and even the cows—than his matchmaking mother and dad. But was that the best way to help them see his point of view? Or grow closer to God?

"Okay, Lord. You win." He tried not to roll his eyes. "I'll apologize for pitching a fit. I'll be nice to this girl on Sunday, since I said I'd meet her. But You know how I feel, don't You?"

After he finished the chores, he remembered Jesus once had been a single thirtysomething. Had His mother tried to marry Him off, too? Kyle had never thought about it before.

He felt strangely comforted as he trudged to the house, hoping to avoid round two.

"At school Madison said she's skied on a mountain in Michigan." Ethan stuffed mashed potatoes into his mouth. "I told her the picture didn't look like a *real* mountain. Not like the ones we climbed with Dad."

"Close your mouth while you're eating, please." Lauren wished she could close her son's mouth at school as well. Ethan, like Brent, never met a stranger. And like his dad, he said what he thought, which his listeners did not always appreciate.

She made herself eat, though she felt more weary than hungry. Filling out job applications online shouldn't tire her so. *You're getting spoiled.* The past two weeks, she'd grown accustomed to Uncle Horton's jovial help at mealtimes. But after the Labs chewed up his favorite slippers, even he had endured enough dog-and-boy disruption, fleeing to a downtown café for supper with a friend.

She glanced at Logan, whose barely touched dinner evidenced something was bothering him. "How was your day, hon?"

"Okay." He looked past her, as if the sodden, gray-brown landscape out the lacy-curtained dining room windows fascinated him. "Can I go now?"

"Are you feeling sick?" Her throat constricted. Was this the beginning of flu? Another asthma attack? She felt his forehead.

"He's always sick," Ethan scoffed.

"Am not." Logan surprised his brother with a punch that nearly knocked him off his chair. Ethan clobbered him back, and the Labs awakened from their living room snooze to charge into the fray. Lauren sent the raging boys to separate rooms and dragged Twinkie into the bathroom and Dinky into the mudroom, where they proceeded to bark themselves hoarse. She surveyed the damage and slowly sopped up Logan's chocolate milk, which had been broadcast everywhere. Beautiful antique table, worn patterned carpet, even the white plaster walls... Lauren would have covered her face with her hands if they hadn't been wet and sticky.

She didn't need a coffee break or even a Beverly Hills spa. She needed a transfer to another planet. The one for runaway mothers.

How would she survive a lifetime of this? She covered her face anyway. *A lifetime? Lord, help me make it through this day.*

No angel with a mop showed up. So Lauren did a preliminary emergency cleanup while trying to decide how to handle the situation. Logan had initiated the physical conflict, but Ethan had baited him.

A mental replay of the dark circles under Logan's eyes sped her movements. She washed her hands, grabbed a thermometer from the kitchen first-aid kit, climbed the stairs to the boys' bedroom, and rapped on the door before entering.

Logan, sitting on the floor playing with Legos, didn't look up.

"Son, I need to take your temperature."

She sat down beside him. "Did you feel bad at school today?"

He paused. "I always feel bad at school."

Her breath caught in her throat. "Logan, are you having trouble understanding the teacher?" *Should I give her a call?*

He shook his head. "I'm okay."

"Okay" for Logan meant top scores. Lauren couldn't recall anything unusual as she mentally scrolled through his homework grades. "Then what's the trouble?" A rush of mom wrath boiled up in her stomach. "Is someone being mean to you?"

"No." He fiddled with his Lego skyscraper. "I don't know anybody. And I miss home." He raised solemn eyes. "I like snow, but it's *cold* here. All the time."

"I miss home, too." Her hands hadn't thawed since she crossed the Indiana border. "But Uncle Hort says it won't be long until spring."

She slipped an arm around him and checked the thermometer. "Your temperature's up a little. Are you having trouble breathing?"

"No. I don't have to go to the doctor, do I?" Logan wiggled away from her.

"I don't think so. But you must tell me if you're feeling worse."

He nodded, as if that were exactly what he would do.

Lauren knew better. But she hugged him again, trying to transition to issue number two. "Logan, look at me. No, at me. You should not have hit your brother."

"He was being mean."

"I know. But that does not mean you can smack him."

"I usually don't."

Lauren bit her lip to keep a smile from sneaking onto her face. "Yes. But you still must apologize."

Logan gave her the patient martyr look he reserved for adult insanity, but he nodded.

When Lauren brought them face-to-face in their bedroom for the mutual apology, Ethan showed grudging appreciation for Logan's potent punch. "You never hit me that hard before." Within seconds they conducted an intergalactic attack together on Logan's skyscraper.

Lauren usually demanded her sons perform at least token penance in "helping" her clean up or repair their destruction. But now she scurried downstairs to try to redo the dining room before Uncle Horton returned. How could one glass of liquid cover so much territory? She'd just finished when the tires of Uncle Hort's old Ford truck ground the gravel driveway. When the back door opened, she glued a smile to her lips and began loading the dishwasher.

His boots thudded as he shed them in the mudroom. He opened the kitchen door and used his red bandanna handkerchief to wipe chocolate milk off the wall phone. "Rough evening, Laurie-girl?"

She faced him with an "it's nothing" wave of the hand. "Oh, the boys acted up."

"Dogs, too, I take it?" He let an indignant Dinky plunge past him into the house.

Accustomed to the Labs' noise, she'd forgotten to free them from their prisons. "Oh, my, Twinkie's still in the bathroom." *What if she's eaten Uncle Hort's soap? His towels?* Holding her breath, Lauren opened the door. Twinkie dove between them and headed for the living room.

Lauren entered the bathroom, wondering if other mothers spent ninety percent of their lives conducting damage control. Relief seeped into tears that gathered in her eyes. Apparently Twinkie had taken to heart her earlier punishment for eating Uncle Hort's slipper. As far as Lauren could see, nothing ripped, shredded, or devoured. Twinkie had overturned the trash can, but the toilet paper holder hadn't been touched.

"Thank You, Jesus," Lauren whispered as she scooped up used tissues and old dental floss.

"How about a cup of decaf?" Uncle Hort called from the kitchen. The coffeemaker's burbling complaints and the brew's heavenly fragrance filled the air.

Lauren's mouth watered as she finished her nasty task. Her entire being, even her soul, longed for a fresh, hot cup of coffee, finished at one sitting as most of the civilized world drank it. But that world did not include moms.

The dear old man met her coming into the kitchen.

"Thanks, but the boys need baths." She thought of Logan's weary little face. "They should go to bed soon."

"I'll do bath duty tonight."

Ooh, so tempting. But bending over the bathtub to wash hair? Scrub ears? "They're a handful," she explained. "It wouldn't be good for your back."

"Back, schmack. It creaks, no matter what I do." He poured steaming coffee into one of Aunt Kate's pink china cups. "I've rassled a hundred calves worse'n those two." He carried her cup to the living room.

"You come up and kiss them good night. But right now, have a seat right here"—he patted his saggy recliner next to the fireplace—"and I'll get those desperadoes cleaned up in no time."

"You two behave yourselves," he told Twinkie and Dinky, scratching them behind the ears. They dropped in front of the fireplace as if Lauren had worn them out.

She gave him a big thank-you hug then sank into the chair. Toasting her toes in front of a glowing bed of embers, she sipped coffee with a long sigh of ecstasy. Someday soon she hoped to ponder the possibilities of her new life.

Of course, she'd have to find a job. She'd always worked in restaurants, and she enjoyed it. Surely someone here needed her skills—whether Californians or midwesterners, people liked to eat out. Since the boys were born, she hadn't thought much about it, but the dream of owning her own restaurant had always lived quietly in a corner of her mind.

Right now, though, sitting was a dream fulfilled. Sitting and finishing this rich, steaming cup of coffee.

Chapter 3

It's her. The basketball game woman. She'd invaded his Sunday school classroom like a lovely special effect in a movie.

Hort Hayworth introduced them. "Lauren, this is Kyle Hammond. He and his family have been good friends for years. Kyle, I'd like you to meet my niece, Lauren Pellegrino. She's just moved to Peru from California." Hort motioned to the two look-alike boys beside her, one trying to shake off his mother's right hand, and the other clutching her left. "And these are her sons, Ethan and Logan."

He could tell she recognized him, too. Rats. "Um, we've met. I was the one who dumped a drink down her back the night we beat Warsaw."

"Hey, I have kids. I'm used to a few surprises." She gave him a knockout smile, but her big, brown eyes looked worried. Separation anxiety? At their age?

He didn't want to shift his gaze from her face, but he knew he could lose control of these third-grade boys in one and a half seconds. He cast a quick look at her ringless left hand, then threw a glance over his shoulder at the dozen arm wrestlers at the table behind him. "Guys, you've got exactly three minutes before you tell me your next verse. Remember April Fool."

Worked every time. For at least ten seconds. Maybe fifteen. He turned back to the visitors. "Hey, glad to have you here with us, Ethan, Logan." He bumped knuckles with each boy. "Which one is which?"

"I'm Ethan." The bolder kid's eyes gleamed with curiosity. "What was that about April Fool?"

"It's a contest. Every guy who memorizes Ephesians 6:14–17 from the New Testament by April first can throw a pie in my face." Kyle grinned. "You look like you've got a good arm."

The kid flexed it. "I play shortstop in Little League. At least, I used to."

Kyle turned to the other boy. "And you're Logan."

Round blue eyes almost looked through him. "Yeah."

So, a quiet one. And probably brighter than most. Kyle went with his gut. "You good at memorizing?"

A small smile crept across Logan's face. "I know all fifty states and their capitals."

Kyle nodded. "Bet you could remember four verses."

"I can do it, too." Ethan stuck his chin out.

"Well, come in and get started." Kyle handed each a purple memory verse sheet and a cupful of Goldfish crackers. He expected Lauren's glance at the snack. "I always memorize better when I eat. I've found these guys do, too."

He hoped for another incredible grin, but she only said, "Thank you." She told her sons to behave and left with Hort.

He really wished moms wouldn't do that. In boy-ese that expression translated into "Take the place apart." Now her twins would do their best to convince the other boys they weren't wimps.

Sure enough, after Kyle introduced the newcomers, Ethan

lost no time in turning his memory verse sheet into a paper airplane. Kyle grabbed it as it sailed past. "Cool plane, Ethan. Maybe if we finish early, we all can make planes and see whose flies the farthest."

"Yesss!" The boys pumped their fists.

"But we'll have to get on it. No goofing off."

Sudden quiet. Whoa, he'd have to try this again.

He sounded out the harder words in the scriptures for boys who struggled with reading. As he picked up pencils, tissues, and Goldfish from the floor, Kyle wished he could have stolen a few moments talking to Lauren. Something about her drew him, and it wasn't just her slim figure, shining hair, and soft eyes. Maybe when she came to pick up the boys, he could linger with her before going home…. Rats. He'd promised to go out for dinner with his folks. And the Sharps. And their granddaughter. He grimaced. What was her name?

"Mr. Hammond, I can say two verses. You wanna hear them?" The quiet twin lasered a look at him, as if he could read his mind.

Already? "Uh, sure." His face grew warm. *Sorry, Lord.* He had no business thinking about women or parents or dinner when he was supposed to be helping kids learn God's Word.

Logan missed a few words of verse eleven, but he had verse ten down, word perfect. Tanner Schwartz, the reigning Sunday school superstar, watched this newcomer with mingled appreciation and angst.

Tanner nailed the passage, but Kyle, as usual, translated as several other boys created their own versions of Ephesians. Most made progress, however, and the promised paper airplane competition gave them a break. Afterward, Kyle pulled his father's sword from its scabbard. He risked a trip to the hospital in showing it to these little yahoos, but he wanted them to get this scripture. Really get it. "My dad wore this sword when he was in the Marines."

"Wow!" Wide-eyed, they crowded around.

He raised the weapon out of their reach. "This blade can slice your fingers off. But if you're careful, you each can hold it."

His students all grasped the grip and ran their fingers along the scabbard. Kyle held the weapon high as he told them about the sword of the Spirit.

So good to be in church again. The past hectic months had pickpocketed Sundays, along with the rest of Lauren's time with the Lord. Now she reveled in the Good Shepherd Community Church choir's less-than-perfect anthem and the worship time, though she didn't know many of the songs. The older downtown church wasn't as big as the one she'd attended in California. But she felt at home here. How wonderful to praise God with His people. The stories the pastor told reminded her how much God loved her and the boys. Pastor Lyons even told one about Labs. Too bad she hadn't brought the dogs; they certainly could use a little sermonizing.

She'd worried about Logan's adjustment, but when she and Uncle Hort picked up the boys, they both said they liked the class.

She hadn't worn heels for a while and walked carefully as she prompted the boys. "What did you learn today?"

"I touched a real sword!" Logan's face glowed.

"Yeah, and we're going to be in a circus!" Ethan yelled.

She might have to dig to find out the scriptural significance of that. But before she could reply, Uncle Hort steered them to a group of smiling churchgoers.

"Hey, Sam, Lindsey. How's your week gone? I'd like you to meet my niece, Lauren Pellegrino, and her boys, Ethan and Logan."

The walk to the parking lot slowed to a standstill. Uncle Hort waved an arm to at least half the congregation. Lauren met Sam and Lindsey Rhoades and their four little towheaded kids. The Goods. The Sabelhauses. The twins, overdosing on introductions, finally begged to sit in the SUV. By the time she and Uncle Hort followed them, Lauren's face hurt from smiling, mostly because she hadn't done much of that lately. Still, everyone seemed so open, so welcoming. She summoned one more grin when Uncle Hort motioned to people entering the big, silver Buick parked next to them.

"Diana, Bob, Rose, Al, I'd like you to meet my niece, Lauren Pellegrino." He turned to Lauren. "Hon, these are the Sharps and the Hammonds. Special people—especially Rose. She's won the county fair's cookie competition every year they've put it on." His eyes twinkled with mischief. "Except last year."

"You'll never let me forget that, will you, Hort Hayworth." The tall woman with the take-charge air smiled, but her blue eyes snapped. "Just because you won one time—"

He chuckled and changed the subject. "I forgot to introduce you to my great-nephews, Ethan and Logan."

Lauren stepped away from the SUV and beckoned to the twins, but both dived for the floor as if threatened by aliens. She really couldn't blame them. Lauren extended her hand to the carefully coiffed older women. "They're a little shy, being new and all. I'm so glad to meet you, but I'm afraid it will take me a while to learn your names."

They laughed sympathetically, and the tall, sun-browned man—Al?—said, "Nobody can remember names like Hort. I think he knows the name of every cat, dog, cow, and pig in Miami County."

"Remember most of the chickens, too," Uncle Hort deadpanned.

Lauren chuckled, but Kyle Hammond, her boys' Sunday school teacher, walking up to the truck on the other side of the Buick, drew her eye.

So did the sleek, striking brunette at his side.

She'd noticed earlier he didn't wear a wedding ring. But, of course, he was married—how could she have thought otherwise? A good-looking guy like that who seemed to love God and little boys. Why did she feel like a rag doll that suddenly lost her stuffing? Lauren's cheeks heated as if the sun were out. Why had she spotted the ring's absence in the first place?

"Kyle, I haven't met your friend." Shaking hands, Uncle Hort almost jiggled the young woman off her stilettos.

Kyle did the honors. "Hort, Ms. Pellegrino, this is Jennifer Sharp—"

"Jenna." The girl's smile tightened in her perfect-tan face.

"I'm sorry. Jenna." Kyle looked less rattled when he'd poured the soda down her back.

So he wasn't married. So what? His date looked stunning.

"Jenna's our granddaughter from Fort Wayne who's visiting this week. Sorry to rush off, but we're trying to beat the Sunday crowd at the Grill." Diana Sharp offered a gracious cutoff to the conversation.

Relieved, Lauren slipped into the SUV's passenger side. The boys, who had discovered Kyle's presence, hooted and waved from the window they'd opened. "Mr. Hammond! Over here! Look at me!"

Logan made his favorite zombie face, his eyes rolled back in his head. Ethan did his triceratops imitation with both thumbs up his nose.

Lauren laid her head on the backrest and closed her eyes. So much for a quiet, understated departure.

"Just how does that contraption work?" Uncle Hort watched Lauren clip the Skype camera to his computer.

"It's not complicated. Even I can do it." She laughed and brought up the program she'd installed. Lauren knew Uncle Hort really missed his only daughter, who now lived in Seattle. "Please feel free to use it to talk to Angela and her family."

"I'll watch you and see if I can get the hang of it." He hustled the Labs out of the cramped computer room and settled them in the living room.

She wasn't sure she wanted him to watch her first extended encounter with her mother-in-law. The Lord knew she initiated this only because she promised the boys they could stay in touch with their grandmother.

"Logan! Ethan!" she called up the stairs. "Come talk with Grandmamma!"

Tennis-shoe thunder rumbled overhead as the twins raced down.

"Wonderful, what you're doing to keep them in touch with her." Uncle Hort beamed at Lauren as if she were Mother of the Year.

As she tapped the keyboard, Lauren felt a little ashamed. Certainly the Lord knew her motives weren't completely pure. Perhaps if they Skyped with Marian on a regular basis, she wouldn't come for a visit. At least, not right away.

Maybe Uncle Hort's presence would work some magic. If Marian knew he was observing the exchange, perhaps she would withhold the barbs she'd used in their brief phone encounters: "Logan, Ethan, I miss you so much. I've cried every day since you left. I'm all alone now... ."

Lauren doubted that very much, which was one big reason she moved to Indiana. Oh-so-devoted Preston probably would hover in the background.

"Where's Grandmamma?" Ethan's eager voice stopped her shudder. The twins plopped onto the stools she'd arranged in front of the computer.

"I'm bringing her up." Lauren smoothed their curls and straightened their collars. Marian's dark, aristocratic face appeared on the monitor, wreathed in smiles.

"Ethan, Logan!" Genuine joy overflowed in Marian's face.

"Grandmamma!" The little boys almost bopped heads, trying to touch the screen.

Marian reached a perfectly manicured hand to them, too. "You both look like you've grown already."

The boys babbled on about their trip to Indiana, the farm,

even school. To Lauren's relief, they mentioned mostly things they liked about their new home. Marian seemed on her best behavior, too. *Long may it last, Lord.*

Lauren intentionally timed the Skype session a half hour before the twins' bath time in order to limit it. Now, if she could gracefully end it...

"Boys, you've got school in the morning. It's time for bath and bed. Throw Grandmamma a kiss."

Though they considered themselves too big for such mushiness, Ethan and Logan complied. Marian threw a half dozen their way. Lauren steered the twins toward Uncle Hort, who headed them up the stairs.

"Thanks for Skyping with us, Marian." The session had surpassed Lauren's best expectations. She shouldn't have given in to such negative thinking—

"Have you found a place to live, Lauren? A job?" No more warmth in Marian's voice.

"Not yet. But I'm checking into several possibilities."

"You could have continued living with us without uprooting the children. And as for jobs, everyone knows about the poor outlook in the Midwest."

"Not many sushi bars in Peru, Indiana, I imagine." Preston's long, pale face appeared behind Marian.

Cringing, she tried to think of an answer.

"True, but this girl's got lots going for her." Uncle Hort, a big smile in his voice, had slipped behind her. "Aren't those boys something? Hasn't she raised them well?"

A pause. "They—they are wonderful children."

What else could Marian say? A giggle wiggled in Lauren's throat, wanting out. She planed her voice to normalcy. "This is my Uncle Horton. You remember, we're staying with him—"

"Most fun I've had in years," Uncle Horton said. "Speaking of which, we'd both better see what those desperadoes are up to. Nice meeting you."

" 'Bye." Lauren quickly ended the session. She felt as if she'd been scrubbing walls again.

"God has good plans for you, Laurie-girl." Her uncle gave her a hug.

Feeling his strong arms around her, she wanted to believe it.

Chapter 4

"Please let us be in the circus, Mom." Ethan knew how to use those big blue eyes. But Lauren had no idea what he was talking about.

"Yeah, Mom." Logan joined in the assault. "Please, please, please—"

"What circus?" Lauren poured chocolate syrup into the boys' after-school milk—the only way they would drink it.

Ethan stirred his at mixer speed. "The one I told you about Sunday after church."

Floating among a hundred new names and a mental image of Kyle and Miss America, she salvaged her son's out-of-the-blue remark about a circus.

"When is the circus coming to town?" Her heart sank. With no job yet in sight, she couldn't afford a splurge like that.

"It's not coming to town, Mom. It's already here." Logan summoned his be-patient-with-the-dumb-adult expression. "Everybody's talking about trying out."

"Yep, it's Circus Roundup time!" Uncle Hort, hauling in

bags of groceries, added to the boy chorus. "Don't you remember it from when you were a girl?"

After filling out applications all day, she was expected to have a brain? "You mentioned a circus in July. But I always visited in August because of my parents' work schedule."

"This is no ordinary circus." Uncle Hort plunked the groceries on the kitchen table and threw out his long arm with a ringmaster's flourish. "Lad-eez and gentlemen! Welcome to Peru, Indiana, home of the Greatest Show on Earth!"

The boys erupted in cheers, hopping around like kangaroos. This time Lauren grabbed their milk glasses before another chocolate tsunami hit the walls. Uncle Hort was stirring up excitement about nothing. She couldn't pay for gas, let alone tickets. Irritation lodged in her stomach like a hot stone.

"Boys, I'm not sure we can afford this." She tried not to glare at her uncle.

The twins dropped to the carpet with a moan.

"That's all we ever hear," Logan muttered.

"If Dad were still alive, we could afford it." Ethan, sticking out his chin, threw a glare of his own at her.

Not necessarily. But he'd take you to the circus, anyway, wouldn't he? She bowed her head.

"I'm sorry to have upset you, Laurie-girl." Uncle Hort patted her taut shoulder. "We're not talking about a regular circus. In the Peru Youth Circus, the children of the town perform."

Her mind dredged up a long-ago conversation or two. She recalled something about child jugglers and tumblers. That didn't sound too dangerous. But nothing was free anymore. Nothing. "Won't that cost as well? Maybe even more than circus tickets."

"Some acts require special clothing," Uncle Hort admitted. "But the boys have had their school physicals, haven't they? So no doctor costs."

Logan's lip trembled. "Mom, everybody's going to be in the circus—"

"We're not everybody."

"You let us do Little League." Ethan was yelling now. "Why won't you let us be in the circus?"

Uncle Hort said, "We could work something out—"

"No." She fought back tears. "I can't let you pay for everything."

"I won't have to, if you'll listen a moment."

She barely heard him because at the word *no*, the twins exploded in sobs of anguish. The Labs—had they been chewing on something under the boys' beds again?—charged from the stairway, barking, because their young masters were in distress.

"I want Dad!" Logan, stretched on the floor, covered his face. "I want my dad!"

Ethan sat up, an angry flood pouring down his cheeks. "Dad would let us be in the circus. He'd even help us."

Their words smashed into her. Her bones felt splintered, broken.

"I—I miss him, too." Though she'd felt like a mother of three, life without Brent's fun-loving spirit seemed so empty, so colorless. *Oh, Lord, we need You. How many times will we go through this?*

Yet, so far, they'd survived.

She knelt and hugged them close. Twinkie and Dinky plopped beside the sad group, licking faces in sloppy sympathy. When Logan's sobs diminished to an occasional soft hiccup, Lauren gently pushed Twinkie's muzzle away from her. "Okay. *Okay.*"

Her shamefaced uncle had retreated to the far end of the table. "I'm sorry. Actually, I was bringing you good news. I should have told you that first, but I got carried away about the circus. But we can talk about that later."

"Just a *little* later," Lauren told the boys, before another storm brewed. They sniffled. She pulled a tissue from her pocket before Ethan could blow his nose on his sleeve.

"I talked to my friend, Sylvia Williams. She and her husband, Roy, ran a café downtown for years," Uncle Hort said. "He's gone now, and she needs an assistant manager, someone she can trust. When she heard about your work experience in California, she wanted to talk to you." He handed her a note. "Here's Sylvia's phone number."

Slowly Lauren took it. "I haven't managed a restaurant in a while. After the boys were born, I worked only part-time."

"She knows that. I think you'll be a good match for the Sunnyside."

Maybe. Her tired heart, dreary as the early March weather, gave a small leap. How she missed the color green—in several ways.

Ethan pounced on her smile. "If you get this job, does that mean we'll be in the circus?"

"Boys, let's not move too fast." Uncle Horton rescued her. "Your mama doesn't know much about the Peru Youth Circus. You've only heard a little—"

"I heard a bunch at school," Ethan protested.

"At Sunday school, too," Logan added.

A wave of mother-caution swept over her. Brent's stunt career had proved to be a continual nightmare. He only laughed when she worried. Did the children do risky acts in this circus? Her sons would not follow in his steps.

"Let's check out some practices at the Circus City Center." Uncle Hort read her, as usual. "Your mom can ask questions, and you two can see what it's really like to perform in the circus." He grinned. "After she makes her phone call to Sylvia, that is."

Lauren nodded. Her knees shook a little, but she went to the kitchen, picked up the curly corded phone from its wall cradle, and hugged it to her jaw.

"That looks like a big tent." Despite the chilly weather, Ethan stuck his nose out the car window, like Dinky.

Lauren craned her neck. The Circus City Center's cream-colored, tent-like canopy with red trim promised a refuge from the sleet streaking their windows. But not even sleet could dampen the glow Lauren felt after talking with Sylvia Williams. An interview! And Ms. Williams seemed almost excited to meet her... .

Uncle Horton whipped the SUV into a parking spot. "Roundup was yesterday, so things are beginning to stir here at the arena."

"Roundup?" Lauren followed the twins through the door.

"An orientation for kids and parents. But tryouts won't take place for a few weeks. I'm sure Patti here can give you any information you want."

"Hi, Hort." The graying, attractive woman sitting behind a desk gave them a circus-sized smile. "Ready to make those elephant ears? Won't be long until the festival."

"How do you make elephant ears?" Logan stared. "Why don't you make the rest of the elephant?"

Lauren tried not to giggle. "Elephant ears are something to eat, guys—and Uncle Hort makes the best!"

"Mmm." Patti licked her lips. "Every year he makes Hort's Heavenly Elephant Ears for the Circus City Festival and other festivals across Indiana. Big, flat pieces of fried bread, covered with cinnamon and sugar—"

"I like the ones with cherry topping best." Lauren almost drooled. How could she have forgotten his concession stand? As a child she'd occasionally gone with him, Aunt Kate, and Angela to neighboring county fairs, selling the yummiest elephant ears in the world.

"Will you make them for us, Uncle Hort?" The twins started their "please-please" routine again.

Uncle Hort promised a batch of elephant ears the next day.

Patti gave Lauren a folder of materials. "Would you like a tour?"

"I knew you'd show off the place." Uncle Hort grinned.

Lauren and the twins followed Patti down a hallway, past a life-size portrait of fierce lions.

It's only a picture, Lauren admonished herself. Still the animals' glittering eyes and long, sharp teeth resurrected her concerns. "Does this youth circus use animals?"

"None." Patti seemed to understand Lauren's angst. "We make children's safety the top priority."

"No lions or tigers or boa constrictors?" Ethan looked disappointed. Logan didn't.

"We have animals in the parade. Last year gorgeous white tigers rode in the wagons. Here's a photo."

They passed a wall filled with smiling portraits of Miss Circus City Festival winners dating back to 1958. Patti caught Lauren's gaze. "Circuses in Peru go back a long way. For years, the Ringling Brothers and Barnum & Bailey and other top circuses wintered here. Emmett Kelly"—she indicated a bust of the famous clown—"and other celebrities often came here during off-season."

Uncle Horton looked at his watch. "I know it's only fifteen minutes till the museum closes, Patti, but can we take a peek?"

"Sure." She led them inside.

"Man, look at all this stuff!" Ethan and Logan nosed around like inquisitive hamsters.

The museum didn't look large, but pictures and memorabilia filled every square inch.

"What's that?" Logan cocked his head, studying a large, yellow wooden sunflower with four clowns surrounding a brown badger-like animal in overalls.

"That used to decorate the music box on top of a carousel—you know, a merry-go-round with lots of horses." Patti touched the badger's nose. "Have you ever ridden one?"

"We went on a giant one with Grandmamma at Six Flags," Logan answered. "I liked the big white horse best."

Patti gestured toward rows of brass tubes and a keyboard.

"Those played whistle-like music. They once were part of a calliope that appeared in circus parades."

"I bet that played loud!" Ethan pointed to an enormous tuba, its bell sitting on the floor.

"Look, boys, here's an elephant collar. And a whole circus train." Lauren knew she'd better steer the twins away from the tuba before they decided to find out just how loud it played.

Uncle Horton volunteered for child duty, so Lauren wandered a little. The vintage costumes—largely ignored by the boys—grabbed her imagination. Gold and blue velvet jackets with rows of silver buttons. A long, black velvet cape with gold curlicues. A little girl's tutu, all pale-pink ruffles, and tiny ballet slippers. Stunning satin headdresses adorned with pearls, silver braid, and shimmering silver coin-like decorations. Some of these, the placards said, belonged to performers who had retired in Peru and donated their costumes.

"Ready to climb on a horse and ride bareback into the ring?" Uncle Horton had slipped up behind her. "Or walk across the high wire?"

"I don't think so." She tried not to imagine looking down.

Dozens of contemporary photos of performers reminded her of Brent's job. All that high wire and trapeze stuff made her want to grab her children and take them home.

"Somebody's probably juggling or working out on the unicycles in the arena," Uncle Hort said. "Can we go check it out?"

He sounded eager as a boy. How could she say no? "All right. Let's do it."

"Yay!" The boys rocketed after Uncle Hort.

She jogged behind, as usual. With kids, who needed Zumba?

"This way." He led them to a set of bright red double doors. White letters proclaimed: "The Greatest Kids in the World Pass Through These Doors. Circus Kids!"

Entering, the twins halted in their tracks, big-eyed, and for once, unmoving.

The huge, gray arena, its high ceiling hardly visible through a network of wires and rigging, echoed with endless energy and motion. A row of trampolines lined one wall, surrounded by girls and boys of every shape and size yelling encouragement to those who bounced and soared high above them. Stretching halfway across the arena, a row of teen and middle-school girls wearing leotards hung from their knees on trapezes, while equally long lines awaited their turn. One girl—she couldn't have been more than fifteen—climbed up on another teen's shoulders while she walked a wire about ten feet above the floor. The walker shuddered, and the long pole she carried flapped. Lauren shuddered, too. But the walker regained her balance. The climber slowly rose above the walker's shoulders, hands extended, trying to stand up straight—then dropped like a rock.

Logan and Ethan yelled. Lauren's hand flew to her mouth.

But the climber fell into a safety net. She wiggled nonchalantly across it, turning a somersault as she dismounted.

"That was better," an instructor called. "You'll make it next time, Kaitlyn."

"Waaay cool. I want to do that."

Lauren expected it from Ethan. But hearing it nearly sent her hand to her mouth again.

"It's a great act." While Uncle Horton slapped Ethan's shoulder, he looked at Lauren. "Those girls have practiced circus stunts for years. High wire is for advanced performers. But they started out as beginners, just like you."

"Well what can we do?"

Circus fever glinted in Logan's eye, as it did in Ethan's. And Uncle Horton's.

"All beginners can do tumbling. Some do roman ladders or trampoline, and a few juggle." Uncle Hort paused. "I coached that stunt when Angela was a girl."

"I want to juggle!" Ethan said.

"Me, too." But Logan didn't sound as positive. Lauren knew he was thinking about Ethan's superiority in Little League. Ethan always played shortstop or first base. Logan inevitably played in right field.

"Like I said, you can try several stunts. You might surprise yourself." He ruffled Logan's hair. "But if you want to try juggling, I'm the second-best coach in the world. Over there's the best, bar none."

A tall guy, trailed by boys and girls carrying what looked like silvery blue and green bowling pins, waved at them across the arena.

Kyle Hammond.

Chapter 5

Her again.

Kyle's heart rate spiked.

She must hide some kind of steel within that lovely, fragile frame. The town grapevine said she was a widow. She'd driven clear across the country alone with her children to start a new life; yet her big eyes darted around the arena as if she were lost.

"Hey, Logan, Ethan. Hi, Hort." Kyle gestured to his jugglers, and they began last year's exercises. Walking to Hort's group, he greeted the woman, keeping his voice casual. "Welcome to chaos, Ms. Pellegrino."

"Please call me Lauren." Her knockout smile looked genuine, though she still appeared jumpy.

Ethan tugged on him. "Mr. Hammond, I really want to juggle, and Uncle Hort says you're the best coach in the whole world."

"There's where he's got it wrong, Ethan." Kyle tapped

Hort's arm. "*He's* the best coach in the whole world. I should know. He taught me."

Hort slapped him on the back. "Kyle could have gone professional if he'd wanted."

"You could have performed in a regular circus?" The admiration in Lauren's voice made him want to show off like a fourteen-year-old. But he detected something else. Fear. What was with that? He wished he knew so he could chase it away.

"I really, *really* want to learn." Ethan interrupted his ponderings.

Kyle liked the determined way the kid set his jaw. "How old are you?"

"Eight."

"I'm eight, too." Logan finally spoke up.

"Do you want to juggle?" Kyle smiled down on the boy, who lifted his chin.

"Maybe."

"I'd be glad to teach you—if it's all right with your mom."

Lauren hesitated. "They wouldn't do anything dangerous, would they? No walking on high wires?"

"Oh, Mom." The twins spoke and rolled their eyes in unison.

"They'll get hit with beanbags or Hacky Sacks." Kyle grinned. "That's what beginners use when they practice. Eventually they'll use clubs—which sometimes smack jugglers in the face." He nodded toward his busy group. "But they try clubs only after they've developed major coordination."

"Those guys have dropped only two or three clubs." Logan's voice held awe. "Can we watch them awhile?"

"Sure." Kyle pointed to Jesse and Mac, who, conscious of an audience, were tossing every third club under their legs then high into the air. "That's called a flourish. Form a triangle," he called to his head jugglers, and Jamie, a middle-school girl who'd made progress since last year, joined in tossing clubs back and forth between them.

"Now let's do a round-and-round." He picked up three metallic-blue clubs and paired himself with Jamie. Jesse and Mac did the stunt almost perfectly, methodically "stealing" clubs from each other as they took turns standing in the front position. Jamie experienced more difficulty, but with a little instruction, she managed a couple of passes in front of him before dropping all her clubs. Her face flamed.

"Good job!" He high-fived all of them and called to the group, "Advanced, the beginners will show up soon. Finish your drills then find the Hacky Sacks and get them started. Intermediates, I'll want to see your newest stunt in fifteen minutes. So do it!"

"Wow!" Ethan was speechless. Almost.

Logan said nothing, but the wonder in the little boy's face inspired Kyle to make them part of his group—and to get to know their mother better. She looked impressed with the jugglers' skills. He gave Lauren his best PR smile. "Taking part in the circus helped me when I was a kid. For one thing, I made lots of friends."

Doubt clouded her face. "But you grew up here. You and your classmates probably were born in the same hospital."

He laughed. "You're right. But I was a big, awkward farm kid from the get-go. And painfully shy—"

"You?" Her jaw dropped.

"Him." Hort nodded. "Could hardly get a word out of him the first week. But after he got into juggling, I thought he'd never shut up."

The twins giggled. Lauren's gaze rested on Logan.

"I learned to have confidence in myself and to work with other people." Kyle gestured with his head toward his jugglers. "These kids work hard. They help and depend on each other—all life skills that come in handy."

He'd given it his best shot, yet uncertainty still simmered in those eyes.

"Mr. Hammond—" Lauren paused.

"Kyle."

"Kyle." That million-dollar smile again. It quickly drooped into an apologetic, almost sad expression. "I—I'm not sure we can afford this. I do have a job interview in a few days that I hope will pan out. But if not—"

"We'll work something out." Kyle finished her sentence. Hort was waggling his eyebrows behind her back, the signal that he'd cover the bases. But Kyle had invented scholarships before, and he would do it again for these kids—and their special mom—if necessary. He knelt down by the twins. "You boys need to be clear on something, though. You're a year or two younger than most beginners. I have no problem with that. But only fourteen jugglers can participate in the circus. First cuts will take place in three weeks. Then second cuts three weeks after that. The chances of eight-year-olds performing in the show the first year are pretty slim. But if you work hard, the odds will look better when you're nine."

"Try out for other acts, too." Hort bobbed his head. "Tumbling, trampoline, roman ladders—"

"I've never heard of a roman ladder." Lauren cocked her head in a cute, quizzical way that Kyle liked.

"Specially adapted ladders are set up on the floor in pairs," he explained. "The boys mostly push them apart, making them open and close as other kids on the ladders do gymnastic poses."

"Just remember, if you participate in the circus, you march in the parade or ride the circus bus and throw candy along the way." Uncle Hort lowered his voice like a conspirator.

The twins' eyes gleamed.

"You *share* the candy," Lauren reminded them. Kyle chuckled.

"*Mom,* I know that." Ethan pushed a curl from his eye. "Do they have clowns in this circus?"

Kyle could see him starring in the clown circuit. "Sure—but clowns can't try out for anything else. They're an entirely separate performing group."

"I'd rather juggle." Ethan bounced as if permanently mounted on a pogo stick.

"Me, too." Logan joined him. "Please, Mom? Let's sign up now."

As they "boinged" around her, Lauren closed her eyes.

"Another great advantage of being in the circus." Kyle, trying to keep a straight face, summoned a deep, solemn tone. "Research has shown that circus practice aids in extricating excess energy from boys, especially during the month of March. These studies also indicate their mothers live longer."

"All right, all *right*." Lauren finally gave in. "We'll work out something. Somehow."

"Yay!" The twins bumped chests, yelling with fierce soprano joy. Lauren shook her head at her sons, Hort, and him, as if they all were impossible boys. But a grin slipped onto her face, capturing Kyle again. He'd dated pretty girls, but her smile squeezed him in two.

He cleared his throat. "We practice Tuesdays and Thursdays at five, mostly in ring one. Do you have time for the boys to join us now? We'll finish by six."

Lauren nodded. Hort looked as if he wanted to "hip-hip-hooray," but he only said, "I need to do some errands. Lauren, you're welcome to go with me or stay here."

"I think I'll watch." She turned and sat on the second bleacher.

"Lots of circus moms in the bleachers at practices," Kyle assured her. "My mother always said she caught up with half the county during circus season."

With a wave to Hort, who headed to the exit, Kyle turned, the two boys at his elbows, ready to spend a busy session with the beginning jugglers.

* * *

Lauren already had lived through three years as a T-ball and Little League mom. She'd been voted Most Likely to Bring Refreshments. But a *circus mom*? The possibility had never occurred to her.

Little misgivings swarmed around her head like gnats in July. How could she have given in so easily? She still didn't know all the facts about the stunts, fees, or costumes. How could she have said yes before nailing down a job? Plus, this place gave her a sense of having stepped into a surreal kingdom. The giant pink polka-dotted balls lined up along the opposite wall and brilliantly colored vintage banners hanging above them only added to the otherworldly feeling—banners featuring Horace the Horse-Man, Jimmy the Giant, Serena the Snake Charmer, and Lilly the Lionface Girl.

What she needed was a good dose of reality. Lauren riffled through the papers Patti had given her. Ah, a stapled xeroxed handbook, application forms, permission forms, physical forms. All the usual stuff that complicated a parent's day. She'd examine them in more detail later.

Far more interesting things were taking place in ring one. Kyle seemed so tall next to the kids. But bending down, he patiently demonstrated techniques to the beginning jugglers: Take Hacky Sack in left hand. Toss only as high as head level. Catch with the right hand. Repeat. Repeat. Now with the left hand. Repeat. Repeat.

Ethan could show surprising patience when pursuing something he truly wanted. The earnestness of his little face made her want to laugh and cry. His coordination appeared better than that of some of the bigger children—and superior to Logan's. Brow wrinkled under his blond curls, her quieter son concentrated with an intensity that begat new qualms in Lauren. What if Ethan qualified in juggling and Logan didn't?

Stop that negative thinking right now. She'd lived through this before. Yes, Ethan would no doubt continue to excel physically, but Logan possessed his own God-given talents. With her help and Uncle Hort's encouragement, he would learn to make the most of them.

Perhaps with Kyle's help, too. She felt herself blushing. Kyle, with his good looks and charm, had accomplished what neither Uncle Hort nor the twins had achieved: obtaining her consent. She hoped no one noticed her red face. Looking around she realized she needn't have worried. These red, green, and yellow bleachers teemed with adults conversing, texting, helping children with homework, chasing after toddlers. The familiar empty "I'm a stranger" feeling swept over her. How she missed Ellie, her best friend back in Los Angeles. But she reminded herself that this circus-mom thing might work out for her as well. Perhaps somewhere in these stands sat a woman who could become her friend. Before long, they'd laugh and talk while sharing a snack and watching their kids becoming circus performers.

She sniffed hungrily. The place smelled like a movie palace, buttery-popcorn good, the fragrance drifting from a big red, white, and blue circus wagon labeled Commissary. She had to save pennies right now, so she steeled herself against the twins' inevitable pleadings after practice. But if her interview Wednesday morphed into a for-real job…

Uncle Hort dropped to a seat beside her and handed her a plastic Subway bag. "Chipotle chicken and provolone on Italian bread, all veggies except green pepper. Did I get it right?"

"You didn't have to do that." He'd remembered exactly the sub she'd ordered last, down to the last detail. Why hadn't some sweet lady latched on to this thoughtful man? She unwrapped her sandwich. "That other bag smells like meatball subs." The twins' favorites.

"Juggling makes a fella extra hungry. They'll be ready for foot longs tonight." Uncle Hort bit into his own roast beef then stopped to wave at a freckled, copper-haired woman about

Lauren's age pushing a stroller past them. "Hey, Julie, come 'ere. Got someone I want you to meet."

"Hi, I'm Julie Tabor." The woman extended her hand. The baby in the stroller flashed a grin nearly as big as her mother's. "This is Maddy. And you must be Lauren, Hort's niece from California."

"That's me." Lauren was learning that Peru's small-town grapevine far surpassed any social network she'd ever joined. "Do you have a child in the circus?"

"Two. Actually three, counting me, which I always do, since I plan never to grow up." That bewitching, slightly snaggletoothed smile again.

"I didn't know adults could participate."

"They help behind the scenes in a million different ways—trainers, costume helpers, band members. My girlfriend Dee plays the oboe. She's performed in the circus band since high school." Julie scooped a fidgety Maddy out of the stroller and gave her a *mmm-waa* kiss. "But since I can't play anything but the radio, I became a security guard—until I got hooked on clowning. It's the only way adults perform out front. I love every minute of it."

Without costume, makeup, or squirting flower, Julie made her feel like smiling. *I'll bet nobody in the world could be a better clown.*

Uncle Hort paused between bites. "Why don't you give it a try, Laurie-girl?"

Lauren nearly dropped her sub between the bleachers.

"Why not? We'll start our practices in a week. You'd have a lot of fun." Julie's cheerful, relentless grin almost made Lauren feel like filling out her own application. But she'd always been the quiet one, never comfortable in Brent's Tinseltown world. "No way. I'm not good in front of a crowd."

"Might be hard since you're brand-new to the area," Uncle Hort conceded.

"Moving so far isn't easy," Julie agreed. "Maybe now's not the right time."

Absurdly, Lauren felt a little disappointed. And panicked that she might not see Julie again. But her new acquaintance's next words reassured her.

"I'll see you here at practices. With two kids doing three or four stunts, I live here during circus season. Though we stopped using sawdust when this arena was built, we still call our circus addiction 'getting sawdust in your bones.'" Julie patted her arm. "It's awfully contagious, so don't be surprised if you catch it, too."

Chapter 6

A bell jingled above the thick glass door Lauren opened the day of her interview. She fell in love with the Sunnyside Café on sight. Even if she hadn't received a job offer, she would have had to return often. She and the Sunnyside belonged together.

Years before, Lauren worked in a small but chic '50s diner. She never expected to encounter real retro in downtown Peru, Indiana. Gray laminate tables and red vinyl chairs against a black-and-white checked tile floor. A polished, old-fashioned soda fountain. Authentic Elvis, Doris Day, Bing Crosby, and Judy Garland albums adorned the walls. The shiny red and black jukebox, embellished with plenty of silver chrome, was no replica. Granted, most of the café's vintage background music emanated from a sound system, but once a month on '50s Night, Sylvia told Lauren she allowed customers to play scratchy for-real records for a nickel apiece. What fun! The perfect job.

Although working the soda fountain might change that.

Her passion for crayfish sushi back in Los Angeles never threatened her waistline. Lauren pressed a whipped-cream can's nozzle, topping turtle brownie sundaes with large rosettes. Tess, the friendly, curly haired server finishing her early shift, whispered that the mayor and two businessmen in booth number seven must have decided to make their afternoon meeting a little more fun. Lauren's stomach growled in protest when she handed over the yummy concoctions to Tess and watched their rapid demise.

Look, you, forget it. You ate a turkey sandwich for lunch; you are not eating a sundae today, even if Uncle Hort says you're too skinny.

Lauren fizzed herself a diet cherry soda. She slipped her phone from an apron pocket, forcing her thoughts away from ice cream as she recorded needed supplies of paper goods. Some people would find this work boring, but taking care of details ensured a smooth-running operation. An efficient, pleasant atmosphere helped tired, hungry people relax. Her mind clicked "before" and "after" pictures of customers each day to admire later. Serving others' needs would never make the headlines, but serving was one of the things she enjoyed most about restaurant work.

She wanted to leave the café in tip-top shape when her shift ended. A few contented-looking customers chatted. Squashed french fries and ice cream sprinkles carpeted the floor under an empty booth where a family with small children had celebrated a birthday. Before "Clean it up!" registered on her mind's monitor, she grabbed a broom and swept them into a dustpan. *Just like home.*

Two guys read newspapers at the counter. Tess filled their chunky red-and-white china cups with the Sunnyside's legendary coffee then gathered ketchup bottles from the tables and took them to the back. Lauren wiped down the stainless steel soda fountain, freezer tops, counters, and garnish station. They gleamed back their gratitude.

Finishing up, she cast a glance over the café, telling the Sunnyside a silent good-bye until tomorrow. She lingered a bit, shooting the breeze with her dreams. Wouldn't it be wonderful to own a restaurant like this someday?

Sylvia, a plump seventyish woman with young eyes, bustled through the kitchen's swinging doors. "How's it going?"

"It's going good." *Actually, it's going wonderful.* Of course, new-job butterflies nearly carried her off at first. But Sylvia appeared almost grateful for Lauren's presence, the servers and cooks answered her questions patiently, and many customers chatted as if they belonged to Peru's Welcome Wagon.

Sylvia gestured with her platinum beehive head. "Please come to the back so we can talk."

Lauren's throat closed, but she followed her boss past enormous fragrant coffee urns, the big walk-in refrigerator, and numerous tables that held drying, floury sheets of the Sunnyside's homemade noodles. She took care not to brush against Tess's ketchup bottles. They lined the narrow hallway to Sylvia's office—half of them balanced upside down on the others, bright red contents dripping into the bottom bottles. Sylvia entered her tiny everything-in-its-place refuge. Lauren slid into a bright yellow chair wedged between a window and Sylvia's desk.

Sylvia didn't shut the door—a good sign.

"You're doing a wonderful job. I'm so glad Hort told me about you." Sylvia's warm words left Lauren limp with relief. "I do need to discuss your hours with you, however. Our most experienced cook is moving to Indianapolis, so I'll play Julia Child until we can hire a new one." A frown lodged between her plucked eyebrows. "I know the early shift works best for your family, but for a while, do you think you could come midday from eleven until seven o'clock on Tuesdays and Thursdays?"

"Sure. I'll work it out." How could she say no? Lauren hated to push afterschool child care and transportation on

Uncle Hort. But she didn't know anyone else. Logan, especially, would not take to a stranger.

"It's a temporary change," Sylvia assured her. "But I don't want just anybody back here cooking for my customers. And the new person will need time to learn our menu well before the festival crowds arrive in July."

Lauren nodded. Sunnyside's reputation for homemade chicken and noodles, pies and breads, as well as superior '50s burger-and-fries fare, kept customers coming back.

"Eventually I'll teach you some of our signature dishes. Right now, keep doing what you do." Sylvia's smile burst open like a spring flower. "Let's hope another employee like you walks through our door soon."

"That's the prettiest little girl I ever saw." Hort, who had helped Kyle and his dad with evening chores, pointed at the long-legged filly lying next to Ruby. "But she doesn't take after her mama."

"No, she's almost as dark as Flourish." Kyle closed his eyes, reliving it all. The breech birth finally took place around ten that morning, but Kyle's insides still quivered at the scare they'd experienced. "For a while we weren't sure Ruby or the foal would make it. When she just wouldn't come, Dad finally called in Dr. Randolph."

"Haven't done that in years." Kyle's father shook his head. "But between Ruby and the three of us, we got the job done."

Ruby whickered, as if to say, "That's what you think!" Even after a long, impossible labor, that mare had attitude. But she looked too weary to do anything other than nudge her baby with her nose.

Watching mother and daughter, an almost fatherly flood of emotion surprised Kyle. *If I feel this way about a horse, how will I react someday when I see the woman I love holding our child?* Strange that in all the animal births he'd attended, he'd never thought about it.

After a final look around, Kyle followed Hort and Dad out of the barn, barring the door behind them. What a day. Ruby and her colt. A mix-up on fertilizer orders. A strenuous circus practice during which one kid kept conking Kyle with his clubs. A quick bite to eat then chores again. He breathed a prayer of thanks that Hort heard of their rough night and came to help. Pausing, Kyle tried to inhale the fiery sunset glory silhouetting the windbreak of giant pines behind the barn. *Please, Lord, help me stay on my feet a little longer.*

"You boys needin' help this spring?" Hort leaned against the barnyard gate, shrewd eyes belying his casual tone.

"Maybe." Dad pushed back his black and gold Purdue cap. "We've hired help, but reckon we might use an extra pair of hands during planting."

Reckon we might. Kyle chafed inwardly, but kept his mouth shut. The doctor had urged his father to undergo hip replacement surgery during the winter months, advice Dad promptly ignored. Now, just before farm and circus work would hit peak levels, he experienced the consequences of his stubbornness. Tonight he was trying hard to disguise his pain.

Still Dad kept up the "maybe" masquerade. "You sayin' you're available, Hort?"

"Most of the time. Right now, I'm watching my nephews and taking 'em to circus practice some. Lauren's work schedule isn't set in stone yet."

"Did she get the job she mentioned?" Kyle barely managed to keep interest from invading his voice.

Hort's face lit up. "Sure did. Lauren's worked several days now. Sylvia—you know, down at the Sunnyside—says Lauren's a little quiet, but that girl sure does know how to run a restaurant."

"At practice the other night, Lauren seemed a little cautious, but I imagine she can do whatever she sets her mind to." Despite the raw March evening, Kyle's cheeks heated up.

"You got that right." Hort winked, and a knowing grin

crossed his face. "Girl drove those two kids clear across the country by herself. By the way, how are the boys doing with their juggling?"

Kyle blessed Hort for changing the subject. "Better than I ever expected of two eight-year-olds." He didn't have to fake his enthusiasm. "Both work hard, and Ethan already surpasses some older jugglers. The acorns don't fall far from the family tree."

"You better believe it." Hort thumped his chest. "But all this juggling talk isn't gettin' your crops planted, Al. When do you think you'll be out in the fields?"

They began the annual guessing game. Kyle breathed a sigh of relief. He didn't mind that Hort already had zeroed in on his attraction to Lauren. The old guy lived with his finger on the pulse of the county's entire population. But if Kyle's clueless dad mentioned Lauren to Mom, she'd try to lasso and tie Lauren like a calf. Surefire way to kill off any chance he might have with her.

With the twilight, Dad invited Hort inside for a cup of coffee. They trudged to the house then shed their mucky boots and jackets. Mom rewarded them with freshly baked apple pie. The kitchen conversation safely centered on seed, rainfall, last year's soybean and corn prices. Kyle ate a lot and said little. His mind wandered back to the twins' mother—Lauren at the circus arena, the Sunday school classroom, even the church parking lot where he'd stumbled and stuttered, back to the basketball game disaster, when those big brown eyes first knocked him off his feet. *Lord, what is this? I don't even know her...but I'd sure like to.*

By the time Hort went home, Kyle had mentally diagrammed new possibilities to keep his path crossing hers. He wouldn't breathe a word about it tonight, but perhaps Hort could use help with the boys, something Kyle wouldn't mind at all—after he got more sleep.

Chapter 7

Four grinning kids riding unicycles shot through the circus arena's back door, zooming past Lauren and the twins. She threw her arms out and flattened the boys against the wall. Would they make it to the practice alive?

After the cycling parade passed, the boys dashed into the huge room and found Kyle, who handed them Hacky Sacks for juggling warm up. Lauren sat in the bleachers, trying not to play helicopter mom, trying not to worry about the cuts ahead. On the plus side, even her shy son mixed with the other jugglers as if they'd known each other forever. Kyle was right. The circus could play a key part in the boys' acclimation to Peru.

Julie, the red-haired clown-to-be, threw Lauren a grin, warming her heart. Lauren waved back. Julie ambled toward her, stopping to gab with everyone. She unstrapped Maddy from the stroller, plopping the baby onto her lap as she dropped beside Lauren.

"Your kids are naturals. Especially that one." Julie gestured toward Ethan. "I haven't seen him drop those Hacky Sacks yet. Are you sure he doesn't have a third arm?"

"I thought both twins did when they were babies." Lauren laughed. "Taking them to the grocery guaranteed excitement."

"I hear you." Julie nuzzled Maddy's plump neck. The baby giggled. "Last trip to the Save-A-Lot, this one shoplifted a little yellow squash and hid it in her diaper bag. Didn't find it until the next day."

Lauren found herself chattering with Julie about their kids. Her facial muscles ached a little. Had it been that long since she'd laughed this much? Julie seemed so relaxed. She barely noticed when her son, Matt, who was the twins' age, fell while balancing a teeterboard on its cylinder.

"He'll survive." She shrugged. "They keep those safety mats under them during practice."

Lauren couldn't help asking, "Do you ever worry about Matt making the cuts?"

"Sometimes." Julie paused then patted her shoulder. "Guess that's part of being a mom, right? But those in charge here do everything they can to include the kids. You'll see."

Just mentioning her angst to someone who understood settled some of Lauren's uneasiness. The nonstop echoey arena noise faded into the background as they talked and laughed. Lauren didn't notice the boys had finished their practice until they popped up at her elbow.

"Hi, guys. You're looking good out there!" As usual, they bounced off Lauren like tennis balls. Hugging them, she peered over their heads. Her heart skipped a beat, several. Kyle—who grew better looking every week—loomed over her.

"Hey, Lauren." He'd finally stopped calling her Ms. Pellegrino.

What a smile. Lauren gave her head a slight shake to break the spell. "Hello, Kyle."

"Hi, Julie. And how's the clown princess?" Kyle tickled

Maddy under her chin. She reached for him with chubby hands. Julie beamed.

This man seemed every kid's best friend. Lauren appreciated that—yet she found herself hoping Kyle's special smile had been for her alone. *Chill, Lauren. You barely know the man.*

Kyle turned to her again. "How's your job going?"

"I love it. The job's wonderful, but the food's too good."

"She brought home a whole peach pie!" Ethan boasted.

"Mmm." Logan licked his lips. "Did you bring one home today?"

"Boys, that pie was an extra. My boss didn't charge me for it. But we won't get a free pie every day—"

"So let's go to Sunnyside and buy one." Ethan turned on his heel. Fearing he would dash out the exit and into the busy street, she grabbed his shoulder.

"My gang will want supper, too," Julie said. "I'd better go meet them at the back door." Waving good-bye, she and Maddy joined the chaos of hungry performers stampeding out of the arena.

"Logan, Ethan, look at me." Lauren tried to corral her twins' attention as other parents and children swept past. "We can't eat pie every night. But Uncle Hort said he would cook spaghetti for supper."

"Yay!" Ethan pulled as if her arm were a leash.

Logan looked like he would dash for the exit any moment, too. As she clutched his shoulder, Kyle's hand met hers. They both jerked back as if they'd touched Uncle Hort's electric fence.

Lauren didn't dare look Kyle in the eye. *Say something. Anything.* "Uh—"

"Your uncle's a great guy." Kyle saved the moment.

She nodded, concentrating on Ethan's dirty face. The boys tugged, anxious as colts to be gone, but she maintained her grasp. "He's been wonderful to us. I told him peanut butter and jelly would be fine tonight, but he wouldn't hear of it."

Kyle chuckled. "He probably wanted spaghetti, too."

His easygoing voice gave her the courage to look up. "He probably did. But I hate to depend on him for—for everything."

"I think Hort's enjoying himself," Kyle said.

A dimple appeared in his right cheek when he grinned. She'd never noticed that before. *You're acting like a teenager, Lauren.* She murmured, "He does enjoy doing things for people, doesn't he?"

"Yep, that's Hort."

"Well, we probably shouldn't keep him waiting." Lauren reluctantly edged her sons through the still-jammed hallway. No hand touching hers. No sizzle this time. But to her surprise, Kyle fell in beside them. Ooh, another sizzle, after all.

"I don't know if you knew this, but Hort's also going to help my dad and me with planting this spring," Kyle said as they moved through the crowd.

She stood stock-still.

A child behind her rammed into her back. As she turned to apologize, Logan, untangled himself from a similar collision and gave her his "Grown-ups!" look. Lauren ignored it. If Hort had promised to help the Hammonds, how would he care for the twins on her late-shift days?

"He told us he would need to stay available for the boys on Tuesdays and Thursdays," Kyle said. "But I have another idea I hope you'll like."

He almost shouted his last words because children and parents, in efforts to connect, yelled and gestured and herded. Lauren felt like she was at a cattle roundup.

Kyle pointed to the sidewalk across the street, and she nodded, as she'd parked halfway down that block. Still clutching the twins, she ducked another unicycle and hurried them out of the crush. *What on earth does he have in mind?*

He didn't keep her in suspense long. "What would you say to the boys serving as my after-practice assistants on Tuesdays and Thursdays? We'll finish cleanup not long before your shift ends. I'll bring them to the Sunnyside for supper."

"Yay! We get to be Kyle's assistants!" Ethan bounced like a kangaroo. Logan pulled his hand from her grasp and high-fived his brother. "Peach pie twice a week!"

"Wait—a—minute, *please*." Lauren's tone halted the celebration. Their cheers gave way to begging then whining. She turned to Kyle, crossing her arms. "That's very kind, but I know you're incredibly busy, especially this time of year."

"I'll be working those evenings downtown, anyway." Kyle's eyes looked almost as pleading as her boys'. "I have to eat sometime."

She pulled her gaze away. *I'm so tired of being helped. I can't let him pay for the boys' suppers. But I can't afford four meals out every week, even with my employee discount.*

She straightened her back. "Boys, please go get in the car while we discuss this."

Ethan started to argue, but Logan yanked his brother toward the SUV.

"Smart kid, Logan," Kyle said softly, as the boys slammed the car doors.

"He knows what works and what doesn't." Lauren chuckled, though she still couldn't look Kyle in the face. "Ethan doesn't always get that."

"I'm sorry I complicated matters by discussing my idea in front of the twins. I should have known better."

She couldn't ignore Kyle's penitent tone. "I appreciate your concern. But—"

"Make no mistake about it. I would put the boys to work."

That deep, firm voice. It not only worked on kids. Her resistance was fading, too. "Obviously they'd enjoy working with you. I know they'd learn a lot." And they'd gain another positive guy influence, besides Uncle Hort.

"It would free up Hort to work with my father. Dad ignored his doctor's orders, and now that it's almost planting time, his hip is giving him fits." Kyle removed his Purdue cap and ran his fingers through his hair. "My mind would rest a little easier, too, if I knew Dad had help while I'm at circus practice."

How could she refuse if this arrangement would aid Kyle's father, as well as give Uncle Hort a break from kid duty? Still, there was the matter of the food expense. "Could we try this on Tuesday next week? To see if it works for everyone?"

"I'll look forward to it." He grinned as if she had done him a huge favor.

Or did that smile, brilliant as a circus spotlight, hold something more?

Chapter 8

"Mom! *Mom!*" Ethan and Logan roared through Sunnyside's glass door, leaving fingerprint smears, startled customers, and a grinning Kyle in their wake. "We did it! We made first cuts!"

"All three events!" Logan almost danced for joy.

"Shhh!" Nevertheless, Lauren plopped down the basket of jellies she was replenishing, scurried from behind the counter, and threw her arms around them. *Thank You, thank You, God, that both of them made it*. She exhaled as if she'd been holding her breath for three weeks. A ripple of applause from the post-dinner-hour bunch surprised her.

"Way to go!" The smiling older couple in booth number seven paused over Beef Manhattan specials to congratulate the twins. The man held up a gnarled hand to high-five them. "Kyle here worked with our grandkids. He'll make you real stars."

A dark-haired, gray-suited woman across from them peered up from her after-dinner coffee and laptop to smile at the twins. "Congratulations. I walked the high wire in the circus when I was a girl."

"Wow, I want to do that, too." Ethan turned to perch at her table. "This year, we're gonna juggle and tumble and do the roman ladders. But I want to try the high wire when I get bigger."

Lauren thanked the lady for her interest with a smile, gently edging Ethan and Logan toward the back tables. Nothing would take their minds off dangerous high-wire stories like food. "Time for supper, guys."

"Get whatever you want." Kyle clapped his hands on their shoulders. "My treat tonight."

He hustled a jubilant Logan and Ethan into a booth and sat across from them.

Handing them old-fashioned menus, she tried to give Kyle a reproachful look but knew she failed utterly. How could she play the strict mom tonight?

He broke down her last objection. "Hey, it's my celebration, too."

He'd certainly earned it, having spent so much time and energy on her sons. "All right. But next time, we're back to the usual."

Not that that stopped him from contributing. He always left her a ridiculous tip.

"Yes, ma'am." He gave Lauren a mock salute as she set water glasses in front of them.

No wonder he got along so well with kids. That big, muscular body housed a boy's heart. *Another boy to raise?* The thought almost sent a slippery glass through her fingers. Brent's face floated through her mind, so close, but out of her reach now. No. She'd already spent one decade of her life with a juvenile for a husband....

Lauren shook herself. Tonight was a special night, a night to smile. She ruffled Logan's hair and asked, though she knew what he'd order. "What'll it be, champ?"

"Tenderloin sandwich and fries. Hold the mayo." He'd learned that listening to Tess put in orders. "I just want dill pickles on my sandwich. And a big, big piece of peach pie with lots of vanilla ice cream on it for dessert."

"And you, champ?" She smiled at Ethan, poising a pencil on her order pad.

"Double bacon cheeseburger with sweet pickles and ketchup. I don't want lettuce or tomato, okay?"

She usually tried to sneak veggies into their meals, but this time, she wrote down as ordered, along with the cherry sodas she knew they'd want. "Fries?"

He looked insulted. "Yeah. And I want the biggest hot fudge sundae they have for dessert."

"Ethan." She hadn't seen anyone finish that sundae. "That's an enormous—"

"I'll help." Kyle volunteered.

She looked heavenward. "I'm sure you will." She shifted a hip toward him. "How about you, sir?"

His glance sent her eyes back to her pad. "Double bacon cheeseburger for me, too. Only I'd like everything on it. Cheese, sweet pickles, lettuce, tomato, mayo, onions—"

"Mom says onions give you bad breath," Ethan interjected.

"Ethan." She needed to finish their order and return to the walk-in to check on dairy supplies for the week.

"Your mom's right." Kyle nodded gravely. "But that's mainly a problem if you're kissing somebody—"

"Yuck," the twins said in unison. Logan crossed his eyes.

Lauren didn't know where to look. "Anything to drink? Dessert?"

"A large strawberry shake with supper, since I may help with Ethan's sundae. And coffee afterward." His eyes almost spoke the question: *With you?*

"I—I'll be back with supper as soon as I can." She whisked the menus away and scurried in a beeline for the kitchen's stainless steel order window. Tess was cleaning out the garnish station. Lauren tapped her on the sleeve. "Will you do me a favor and make a large strawberry shake and two cherry sodas for"—she almost said "my guys," but amended her words just in time—"for the circus boys back there? I need to finish checking the walk-in."

"Sure." Tess shook her head. "But why don't you go celebrate with them? Even Sylvia says you work too hard."

"Yes, Lauren does." Her boss's pink-lipsticked mouth spoke from the window as the burgers sizzled on the grill. "Go ahead. Doesn't look like there's a lot left to do before closing."

Lauren gave silent thanks she couldn't see her boss's probing eyes. "All right, you two, I will sit down—when their food's ready."

She slipped through the kitchen door and zipped past Sylvia before she could say anything more. Almost running to the walk-in, she ducked inside and inhaled its welcome coolness. One deep breath. Two. How many would it take to soothe her heart's *thump-thump*s, as rapid and crazy as the Labs' wagging tails against a car seat? Her own mind was betraying her. Thoughts of Kyle, with that wistful sit-by-me gaze, had followed her into the walk-in, where he had no business being.

She could calm her kids—sort of—and even her dogs, sometimes. But could she collect herself enough to sit next to that kind, gorgeous guy and try to think of him only as her children's juggling instructor?

She could and she would. Another deep breath. Another. *Thump-thump-thump.*

"Why don't you ask my mom to a movie?"

Clubs exploded from Kyle's hands, flying through the air like planes that had lost their radar. "Excuse me?"

No, no, I shouldn't have said that—

"Why don't you ask my mom to see a movie with you?"

As he feared, Ethan yelled the words so half the circus arena could hear. Women tumbling trainers stopped their gab,

casting interested glances his way. If he didn't make this conversation more private, he and Lauren might find their way
into tomorrow's headlines in the *Tribune*. Complete with an
engagement picture.

"Guys, let's go to the bleachers to do cleanup duty." After-school snacks piled up stray papers and cups pretty fast.
He whistled for Logan, who was picking up Kyle's dropped
clubs, then hustled them out of earshot.

"But—but, I thought you were going to show us some of
your best juggling moves," Ethan protested.

"I will later." He handed them each a couple of crumpled
fast-food bags he'd picked up. "If you get the trash from the
bleachers while I clean around the concession wagon, I'll buy
us all a snack."

They zoomed off as if propelled by rocket fuel.

Lauren wouldn't approve of bribery, but working with kids
throughout the years, he'd found it a tried-and-true technique.
Plus, he wouldn't mind a Snickers himself. A man shouldn't
try to figure out a woman without a major sugar charge to his
system. Kyle scanned the area for trash.

How he wished he knew what Lauren really thought of
him. When the boys made first cuts, he could hardly wait to
celebrate with her at Sunnyside.

Not what he expected. Lauren expressed appreciation for
his work with the boys at the circus and church, but nothing
more. She cheered the twins' success and wanted to hear every
detail about their upcoming events, but she said very little to
Kyle. He almost felt like an intruder, as if she would prefer
their little family could share this moment alone.

Why don't I just forget it? He tossed paper cups into a trash
can. Life before Lauren seemed so blessedly simple—full of
hard work, of course, but simple. He'd left behind the world
of dating with its guessing games and endless complications,
decided to let the Lord bring someone special into his life
if and when He planned it. Snapshots of Lauren clicked in

succession through his mind. Laughing with her boys—she looked young enough to be their older sister; surveying her domain at the Sunnyside, all business. He'd stolen glances at church—her eyes closed, a soft flush of color in her cheeks, lips moving in praise and prayer.

Bending down to retrieve ice-cream wrappers and nachos trays, he realized he'd never dated anyone who poured herself into worship that way. It made him want to join her. Suddenly he felt as if a juggling club had struck him on the head. *Did You send Lauren here, Lord—for me?*

"We beat you!" Ethan bellowed in his ear.

Kyle blinked. If he was waiting for an angel to deliver an answer, this wasn't it. Kyle straightened. "Maybe so, but can you do this?" He took several steps back, crushed the nacho trays into a ball, and shot it, three-point style, at the trash basket. "Hammond wins it in overtime!"

"Cool." Logan looked properly impressed. "No way could I do that."

"Can we have our snack now?" Ethan had one thing on his mind.

"Okay." Back from great romantic and spiritual ponderings to the real world. "Hand over your bags and let me check 'em."

He'd learned to monitor their finds before dumping them— more than once, he'd rescued somebody's homework from Logan's obsessive neatness. The boys finished their task in record time, so he slapped down a few dollars on the concession counter and let them choose their favorites. They took Butterfingers to the bottom bleacher to munch while he savored a big Snickers. Mmm. He hoped he never grew too old to appreciate a good candy bar.

Kyle enjoyed all the performers, no matter what their event. He and the boys watched several girls hang by their feet and hands from a network of rigging called the Spanish web. The smallest girl hardly looked twelve years old, the required minimum age to try out, yet the little fairy spun up there, hanging from her loop by one foot, arms spread like wings.

No one in Miami County had to run away to the circus. Here in Peru, Indiana, amid miles of corn and soybean fields, they learned the joy and discipline of doing stunts like professionals. Kyle, relishing the last of his candy, gave thanks again for his community and the people who'd made it happen.

"So when are you going to ask Mom?" Ethan, having taken care of more urgent matters, returned to his original query.

With a twin on each side, Kyle blushed like a cornered teenager. "Uh—it's not that simple."

"Why not?" Logan demanded. "She likes you. You like her. You both like Jesus." His round blue eyes held a no-nonsense expression that would have made Kyle laugh, if he hadn't felt outnumbered.

He hedged, "Those are the important things." He blinked. Yes, they were. The kid had it right. *Thank You, Lord.*

"So ask her to a movie." Ethan wasn't going to let go of this.

"Do you really think she likes me?" He couldn't keep the middle-school note out of his voice.

"Mrs. Tabor—you know, the lady Mom sits with when she watches us—was telling her the other night she should go out with you." Lauren obviously hadn't realized Ethan's hear-all, see-all camera was rolling.

Logan nodded. "Mom turned real red and smiled. Like when Dad brought her roses."

The twins had never mentioned their father. Now he really felt caught in quicksand. Should he encourage Logan to say more?

"But Dad fell off a mountain. He's in heaven now." The little boy dropped his eyes, and Kyle squeezed his shoulder gently. "I'm glad there aren't any mountains in Indiana."

"Mom needs somebody to do mushy stuff for her now." Ethan's one-track mind stayed on task. "So when are you going to ask her to go to a movie with you?"

With this double-powered dating service, Lauren wouldn't last long as a single mom. Maybe he'd better make his move before they trapped another possible suitor. "I'm not sure *when* I'll ask her, Ethan. It's not like making a dentist's appointment. But maybe you guys can help me here. What kinds of movies does your mom like?"

"She says she likes chick flicks." With Logan's disdain, his pensive mood faded.

"She doesn't like cartoons or cool movies with car crashes or fun stuff like that." Ethan shook his head.

"And she doesn't think it's funny when people fall down. She's afraid they'll get hurt." Moms defied Logan's understanding.

"I think I get the picture." Kyle stood. "Hey, you still want to see those tricks I promised?"

Kyle threw his clubs into the air and performed thump spins, surface spins, and chops as the twins watched, open-mouthed. No bobbles, wobbles, or drops. Just a smooth rhythm, each club spinning into his hands then into the air, controllable, predictable. If only his next conversation with Lauren would go so well.

Chapter 9

"*Aaaaaiiiiieeeeeeee!*" Like a wrong chord struck at full volume on a pipe organ, the man's yell reverberated throughout Sunnyside.

No wonder. A platter-sized plateful of chicken and noodles, swimming in hot, creamy broth, had slid off Lauren's tray onto his shoes. As the tray tilted, a basket of oven-fresh rolls flipped skyward then rained down on him and his wife.

Lauren froze. She'd never done this, even at Denny's, her first job. Only in her nightmares.

"Oh, sir, are you all right?" She fell to her knees in the mess, a hundred incoherent apologies pouring from her lips, impotently dabbing at the man's fine-quality shoes and dotting his pants legs with paper napkins. His wife, glaring at Lauren, pushed her aside and took her place.

Like a guardian angel, Sylvia materialized with paper towels, soothing apologies, and offers of free meals and dry cleaning compensation. Her glance, like a gentle elbow in Lauren's side, said, "They're too mad to listen to you. I'll handle this."

Lauren had handled many such situations for those who worked under her. But this time she was the whipped-puppy employee who skittered through the swinging door to avoid a customer's wrath. Her inner GPS directed her to the walk-in refrigerator, which had become her refuge when she wanted to hide from the world. But how could it provide sanctuary for her today?

She entered and slumped against the cold, moist door. The refrigerator's sympathetic hum couldn't drown out the self-smearing epithets roiling inside her. *Stupid, stupid, stupid.*

If only she hadn't tried to help Tess during the busy lunch hour by waiting on some of her customers. That kind of help nobody needed. "Oh, God. Please get me through this day." She thought a minute then added, "Preferably alive."

Perhaps she might have worked through her shift without disaster if the rest of the day had cooperated. That morning the boys wanted to ask Uncle Hort for extra spending money for a school field trip. So inappropriate. Their blank eyes revealed they didn't understand her lecture explaining why. While dressing for work, she discovered Twinkie and Dinky—whom she'd thought were adjusting to their new environment—had shredded a basket of clean laundry, including every pair of underwear she possessed. To top it all off, her weepy mother-in-law called her at work. Trying to keep her temper, Lauren cut her off. But what if she called again? Now this. She covered her face with both hands. Sunnyside's chicken and noodles had been her favorite. Would she ever enjoy them again?

Stacks of fresh butter, eggs, and megacartons of cottage cheese and sour cream filled the shelves. Bunches of fresh carrots, lettuce, and parsley, bags of fragrant apples and grapefruit—she wanted to shove them all aside. Her fingers itched to probe the walk-in's chilly walls, testing each metal panel for a secret passageway. Bolts would loosen, and a door would swing open, an escape to a magic land where children obeyed, mothers-in-law disappeared on command, Labs ate only Purina Dog Chow…and nobody was ever fired from a job.

Would Sylvia let her go?

Don't be silly, her common sense argued. Sylvia appreciated her work. She knew everybody had a bad day now and then.

But what if she does fire me? The words yammered in Lauren's mind like a discount store's blaring loudspeaker announcement. Times were tough in the Midwest. How would she ever find another job? What if she had to depend on Uncle Hort for everything? Kyle would think she was a freeloader, a helpless woman who couldn't cope with life.

Kyle? Though her toes grew numb with the cold, a flush of heat scalded her face. Why did he show up in her thoughts every time she found herself alone or afraid? She needed to get real, here. Men could not save a woman from her problems or her loneliness. She should know that better than anyone. Besides, why would a great-looking guy without a care in the world take a second look at a penniless loser with two kids?

"Enough." With a single word from her Father, the overheated, manic machinery of her mind screeched to a halt.

She drew a slow breath. Another. *I'm sorry, Lord. I'm acting as if You don't exist. As if You've never helped me before.* She discovered she'd clenched her hands into fists. Finger by finger, she released their tension.

Playing Twenty Questions with myself inside a big fridge won't solve much, will it? Shivering, she hugged herself. A good feeling that reminded her she wasn't alone, that God's arms surrounded her, too. Somehow, some way, He would work it all out.

As for Kyle—he was a good man, a kind man who liked her boys. Period. No unrealistic expectations, no romantic fantasies. Letting her imagination run wild like some adolescent would only complicate her life further. And the Lord knew she didn't need any more complications.

The walk-in door creaked then opened.

"Thought I'd find you here." Sylvia stuck her poufy head in. Lauren noticed she'd changed her everyday earrings from big, dangly snowflakes to big yellow tulips. "You can come out now. They're gone."

Slowly Lauren eased out of the shadows. "Do you think they'll ever come back?"

Sylvia laughed. "Charlie Brighton has come here every week for thirty-seven years. He isn't about to give up his chicken and noodles. Another plateful for free, and he almost forgot the entire incident."

Lauren bit her lip. "I'm so, so sorry—"

"Forget it, hon." Sylvia entered and patted her shoulder. "I know you don't normally dump noodles into my customers' shoes."

"Tell that to Mrs. Brighton." Lauren grimaced. "She was pretty mad at me."

"She can get snippy, but when I told her you were working to support your little boys, she quieted down. Actually, she's a kindhearted person."

"I—I just don't want to mess things up for you." Unruly tears threatened to escape her tired eyes. Lauren squeezed them back.

"Gracious, girl, let it go. You've been wonderful since the day you walked in. I wouldn't know what to do without you."

Now she really had to fight tears.

"Let's get out of here before we turn blue." Sylvia shoved the door open. Lauren gratefully followed her out, closing it with a *whumpf.*

"Get yourself some of that fresh brewed coffee and thaw out in the break room for a few minutes." Sylvia's cushiony hug felt like a mom's. Her own mom had been gone for so long, she'd forgotten what that felt like.

"Then come out front. You might find a little surprise there that will give you a smile."

She hadn't the faintest idea what her boss was talking about—maybe another free peach pie?—but nothing could compare with the waves of relief sweeping through her. She filled a mug halfway, splurged on double cream, and gulped it down, its friendly warmth soothing her shivering bones. Thank God and Sylvia, she had a job, and she wanted to perform it to the best of her ability and beyond. For the rest of the day and forevermore, every customer in that dining room would be king.

She flipped her hair from her face, raised her chin, pushed through the swinging door to the dining room—

And halted in her tracks.

"Don't ask for the chicken and noodles today. They might serve 'em to you in your shoes."

Kyle, holding the Sunnyside's door open for Charlie Brighton and his wife, blinked as the old man exited, heh-heh-heh-ing. Mrs. Brighton, however, looked upset. What was that all about?

Kyle entered and sat on the counter stool closest to the kitchen, hoping she'd appear. Wishing she wouldn't. Telling himself he shouldn't have let her kids talk him into making his move too soon.

When Lauren burst through the kitchen door, Kyle thought the paparazzi should be present to capture that smiling face, lovely as a summer day, that shining California gold-streaked hair. When she saw him, however, the glow retreated, as if replaced by the hesitant April sun outside. Smile. Frown. Smile. Frown.

"Uh, hi." Never let it be said that Kyle Hammond didn't know how to charm a woman.

"Hello." She cocked her head in that cute way that made him crazy. "Need some more coffee?"

"No—uh, yeah, I could use some more." He'd been

smoother than this back in middle school. What was it about her that shook him so?

She grabbed the coffeepot from its warmer and poured it expertly into his cup. He wondered how she did that, as his own Mr. Coffee seemed permanently surrounded by spill stains. What he wouldn't give to have her pour it every morning, sunbeams playing with that golden-wheat hair—

She whipped away before he could utter another syllable. Out of the corner of his eye, he watched her smile and talk with a neighbor of his at the cash register. When she poured coffee and laughed with a seed salesman who traveled through Peru during planting season, hot suspicion simmered in Kyle's throat.

The guy's an operator. Stay away from him, Lauren. Before he knew it, he found himself at her side, coffee cup in hand. "So—how's it going, Jason? How are your wife and kids?"

The man blinked. Not surprising, since Kyle had never bought one kernel of corn from him. Jason kept that toothy smile, but his eyes narrowed. "We're good. How about you, Kyle? Heard you were engaged to that Wilson girl over in Wabash."

He heard Lauren's sharp intake of breath. "Not engaged. And we broke up more than a year ago. Almost two years."

She slipped away to seat incoming customers, leaving him and Jason alone. Still facing the other guy, Kyle felt foolish. She'd talked to Jason, but that was part of her job. Maybe he'd jumped the gun, being so nervous about asking her—

"That is one hot woman." Jason's gaze attached to Lauren like Velcro, following her every movement.

A geyser of anger spurted inside Kyle, but he forced himself to lower his voice. "She'll never go out with you."

"Oh, I think she might. She likes me." The man gave him a cool grin that only raised Kyle's inner temperature another hundred degrees. "Besides, whether she does or not, it's none of your business. Who are you, her big brother?"

Kyle's fist ached to smash in those white, white teeth. He gripped his coffee cup with both hands. "I'm her friend."

"Ohhh. Her *friend*."

He turned away and pushed his right foot in front of his left, then moved his left foot. Right. Left. He almost marched himself across the room to his counter stool, fighting the urge to turn sideways again so he could keep an eye on the creep. Instead, he listened. Listened so hard his ears almost hurt.

But Lauren didn't go to Jason's table again. Sylvia razzed the man as she took his money at the register, saying it was about time he got off his rear and went back to work. When the bells over the door jingled his departure, Kyle breathed again. And felt ashamed. Sylvia no doubt had taken in the whole scenario and seen him almost start a fight in her restaurant. He could see himself trying to explain *that* to his Sunday school students.

What had gotten into him anyway? Lauren was not some helpless little girl. She was a beautiful woman who, as that slime Jason had said, might not appreciate Kyle's sticking his nose into her business.

Lauren didn't return to Jason's table. But she hadn't come back to the counter either. Maybe she'd overheard the whole thing and wouldn't ever want to speak to him again.

He shoved several dollar bills under his cup, edged to the door without talking to anybody, and walked out.

Chapter 10

She never wore a dress at home. She'd been a blue jeans girl all her life. Yet Logan slipped into her bedroom, poked his face around the library book that had initiated her unplanned nap, and asked her to change.

"Why don't you wear your yellow dress, Mom? It makes you look happy."

"Yeah, Mom." Ethan popped in, too. "Then you won't look so old."

Ahem. Exhausted did not equal ancient. At least, that's what she told herself. She yawned, stretching her jaws until she thought her head would split. "Guys, I'm too tired to change, okay? Why this sudden interest in my wardrobe, anyway? We're staying home for supper. Uncle Hort's fixing chili."

Logan cocked his head, his round eyes reproachful. "We just like you to look pretty."

Groaning, she fell back onto her cushy pillows, clutching Aunt Kate's soft, worn quilt. Lauren had worked eight days straight because of Tess's illness. Why did the boys hit her

with off-the-wall fashion concerns when she could be luxu-
riating in warm, rare, velvety sleep? "I'll make you a deal. If
you wash your faces and put on those sweaters Grandmamma
bought you for your birthday, I'll put on the yellow dress."

Her eyes still closed, she repressed a not-so-motherly
chuckle as she heard both twins gag and leave. They loved
Grandmamma, but Lauren had barely rescued the artsy mauve
and purple sweaters from the boys' trash can. Did she even
bring them to Indiana? Drowsiness overtook her and swad-
dled her like a baby... .

"Mom. Mom. It's almost suppertime."

Groggy, she thought she had forced one eyelid open. Yet
the scene before her couldn't be real.

Ethan and Logan, wearing the despised sweaters and identical martyrs' expressions, tugged on her. "You said you would
wear the yellow dress, Mom. Get up."

This is one weird dream. She turned over, but the hands
shaking her would not go away. Finally she pushed herself
off the pillows. "Okay, okay. I'm up."

She stretched and hoisted herself to her feet. "I'll have to
find the dress." She pushed past Twinkie and Dinky, who
had parked their haunches in front of the closet. The twins
hovered behind her. "Guys, I don't need an audience. I have
no idea where this dress is. If you want me to find it, take
the dogs and go downstairs. Or, at least, to your own room."

"Okay." They departed, and she returned to her task.

She shuffled through pants, tops, a suit or two. That dress
had to be somewhere in here. Had she even unpacked it? No
way would she dig in those boxes. Oh there it was. Sleeveless.
She sighed. Though the calendar said April, she'd barely given
up her woolliest sweaters. She battled through clingy hang-
ers then dragged the dress out of the back corner. Would it
still fit? Oh, well. The boys wouldn't mind a tight seam here,
a little fold of flab there. She ditched her jeans and slipped
the dress over her head, sucking in her breath before attempt-

ing to close the zipper. She turned to see the dogs still sitting by the door, staring as if she belonged in a circus sideshow.

"So I'm wearing a dress. Get over it." She ran a brush through her hair and zipped lip gloss over her mouth. The woman in the mirror gave a little smile of approval.

"Logan's right. This dress does make me look happier." After all, the calendar did say spring.

"Don't you look pretty!" Uncle Hort paused by the stove, wooden spoon in hand. "Just like the daffodils that'll soon be blooming by the front porch."

"Flowers actually bloom in Indiana?"

He grinned. "Spring's takin' her time getting here, but she's never forgotten us yet." He called to the living room, "Come help put it on the table, boys!"

The twins burst into the kitchen, sniffing the chili-laden air. "Mom, you look awesome!"

She hugged one on either side, glad she'd gone to the trouble. Actually, supper with all these complimentary guys might not be such a bad thing—

A knock at the back door. Instantly the expressions on her three admirers' faces morphed into exactly the same look: a suspicious blend of triumph and mischief, with just a tinge of guilt.

The twins dashed to the door and yanked it open.

"Hi, Mr. Hammond!" They danced around him like ancient aborigines.

Tired or not, she really should have figured this out. Fuming inwardly, Lauren dredged up a weak smile.

The last time she'd seen Kyle—on that awful day at work—he'd said very little, admitted he'd dated some Wilson girl, and left Sunnyside without a good-bye.

Backing against the kitchen table, she didn't want to meet his gaze. Yet how could she avoid it? "Hello."

"Hi, Lauren." He remained near the door as if he wanted to escape, and he looked almost as uncomfortable as she felt.

But wow! The rust-colored shirt, striking against his dark hair and eyes, hugged his broad shoulders and muscular arms. A chilly breeze from outside wafted his aftershave toward her. She wanted to disappear, and she wanted this moment to never end.

"Come in, Kyle. Hope you're hungry." Uncle Hort closed the door.

"I am!" Ethan grabbed Kyle's arm and hauled him to the table.

"Did you fix the chili hot enough?" For the first time, a small smile wriggled from a corner of Kyle's mouth. "Has it burned up the spoon yet?"

Uncle Hort raised his favorite utensil. "Nah. But I think the soup's pretty good. Anyways, it'll have to do. These boys are about to gnaw my arm."

"You guys come and help me make a salad." Lauren needed something to do. Anything.

"I already helped Uncle Hort make it." Logan yanked the refrigerator door open and pulled out the big, crystal bowl.

Fresh-looking greens and veggies, dried cranberries, and sliced almonds sprinkled on the top. Lovely. But Logan with a crystal bowl? She reached—

"I'll take that to the table. You bring the dressing, Logan." Kyle grabbed the bowl and slipped bottles from the shelf on the door. He smiled wider at her surprise. "My mom always taught me to help in the kitchen."

"I'll bring crackers." Ethan grabbed the basket and took her hand. "I set the table, too. Come look, Mom."

Lauren peered into the dining room. Impressive. Aunt Kate's best tablecloth. All the forks on the left side, spoons on the right. Not a single Scooby-Doo drinking glass in sight. Although Uncle Hort and the boys had overstepped her boundaries, how could she not make this a special night for them? Besides—was she imagining it?—she'd intercepted a glance or two from Kyle that made her catch her breath. Did he like the yellow dress?

Uncle Hort followed with an enormous, steaming tureen. Ethan steered her away from her usual chair on the end and tapped one on the side of the table. "You sit here tonight, Mom. See, I drew you a card with your name on it."

"How nice." She peered at the little trapezoid-shaped paper. "Is that a picture of Twinkie?"

He nodded, a proud smile crossing his face.

"I made Mr. Hammond's with a picture of Dinky." Logan pointed to the chair beside her.

"Hey, this is a pretty classy place to eat." Kyle pulled her chair out. "Maybe I should have worn a tux."

A vision of him in evening dress nearly made her miss her seat. He smelled way too good.

"You two might have your pictures on place cards, but you'll eat your supper in the mudroom." Uncle Hort herded the Labs out the back door.

The boys shook the table, and Ethan almost elbowed Logan to keep him from sitting down first, but their efforts to act civilized truly amazed her.

Uncle Hort, sitting on her right, reached toward her. "Kyle, would you say grace for us?"

"Sure."

Kyle's hand swallowed her left. Uncle Hort's fatherly expression clutched at her heart. The boys joined the circle, bowing their blond heads. Before closing her eyes, she snatched a quick look at their reverent little faces. *Father, I am blessed.*

"Lord, we thank You for this wonderful meal. Please bless the hands that prepared it. And help us to be the people You want us to be. Amen."

"Aaaaaaamen!" Logan, who already had readied his spoon for action, dropped it. Ethan fell off his chair.

Well, she hadn't really expected the boys to maintain perfection forever. Uncle Hort and Kyle insisted on serving, filling glasses, and taking care of every minicrisis. Lauren, who couldn't remember the last time she'd eaten a truly hot bowl of soup without interruption, savored every bite. During the meal, Uncle Hort and Kyle entertained them all with circus stories. And when their guest offered her the crackers and cheese at least four times, his gaze held hers as if he didn't want to let go.

The mealtime enchantment continued. *Surely we've set some kind of etiquette record.* Not a single glass of milk spilled. Not a single fight about who ate the most, ate the least, or could burp the loudest. Uncle Horton made supper-time bearable, but Kyle was a genie with the boys. She found herself wishing he could eat every meal with them. At the thought, flames of discomfiture crept up her face.

"This is a wonderful meal, Hort. With wonderful company." Kyle addressed her uncle, but he looked at her.

Chilly arms prickling in the sleeveless dress, she smiled back. Supper with all these courteous, chivalrous guys turned out to be a pretty good thing.

He'd made it through an entire dinner with Lauren without saying something lame. Now Kyle sat beside her on Hort's living room sofa, so close he could count the few faded freckles on her nose.

"Find the movie we picked for Mom, Logan." Ethan's bossy tone beside him broke the spell—at least, a little.

Logan threw his twin a cool try-and-make-me glance, but he pulled a video from the top of the stack under the boxy television. "I put it right here before Mr. Hammond came over." He flipped the old VCR open. "You'll like this one, Mom. Nobody gets blown up."

Kyle recognized the movie's blurry, aging soundtrack. *It's a Wonderful Life.*

Hort cleared his throat. "Actually, boys, that's a Christ-mas movie—"

"It's one of my favorites, and I haven't watched it for a long time." Lauren gave the twins her million-dollar smile.

"Guess there's no law that says you have to watch it at Christmas." Hort pulled the kids' coats from the closet. "Come on, guys. You did a good job helping me with dinner. I think we all deserve a little ice cream—"

"Or peach pie." Logan's eyes glittered.

Hort chuckled—"or peach pie for dessert."

"But Mom won't get any." Logan grabbed his coat, but his conscience wouldn't let him put it on.

"Mr. Hammond won't either."

Ethan stuck up for him. Kyle liked being included in the kid's scope of things. He liked it a lot. But he really didn't need dessert because Lauren sat so close, her still-tanned arms and throat contrasting with that yellow dress, all banana-cream-pie delicious.

"Don't worry about me, boys." She stood, and the twins gave her bear hugs. "I ate so much chili I don't think I could eat another bite."

"I'm good, too." Good? Wonderful was more like it. Lauren could have manufactured a yen for pie. But she wanted to watch a movie alone with him?

"I think your mom and Kyle will find their own sweetness." Hort—at heart as ornery as his nephews—winked as he handed them the remote and steered the boys toward the door.

"What's that mean?" Logan's words floated, loud and clear, from the driveway.

Kyle squashed a laugh. He didn't dare look at Lauren, so he watched the cheesy movie intro portraying God and heaven. It was his least favorite part.

"The theology's a bit off, don't you think?" Lauren's big brown eyes peered at him sideways, her blond head tucked into the fat padding of the flowered sofa.

Oh, he wanted to kiss her. Just once.

Once? Who was he kidding?

Aloud, he said, "Agreed. That aspect isn't accurate. But taken as pure entertainment, it's a fun movie."

She gave him one of her sun-smiles and focused on the video as if someone were going to give a quiz. Her intensity. That was one of the things he loved about her. Right now, it also made it possible for him to study her: the long, dark lashes that fringed her eyes; the curve of her gold-wheat hair toward her cheek; the full, ripe peach slice of her mouth—

He really should pay more attention to the movie.

But the present scenes did nothing to dispel his mood. George Bailey, newly entranced with his old chum's pretty sister. George Bailey, singing "Buffalo Gals" to Mary in the moonlight. George Bailey, coming home for the first time to his beautiful bride—

A light touch on his right pinkie nearly sent him through the ceiling. Barely in time, he kept himself motionless—a woodsman skill he'd learned in Boy Scouts years ago. Another feather touch. He dared cast a glance down. Lauren's left hand now lay beside his, with only a thread's breadth between them.

He edged it toward hers until a long, soft line of her skin touched his. She did not move away. He slid his palm under her hand. Her small fingers curled around it.

On the screen, Bert and Ernie, as if cued from Kyle and Lauren's personal script, warbled, "I Love You Truly." He would have loved to have sealed the moment with a Hollywood kiss or two—or three—or four.

Take it slow, Hammond. Slow and easy.

Instead, he luxuriated in the hand-in-hand closeness and the wonder of the smile they shared before both turned back to watch *It's a Wonderful Life*.

Lauren, snuggled in her quilt, tried to read the library book again, but this time she couldn't fall asleep.

How could she have misread Kyle so?

For after Uncle Hort and the boys returned and retired, she and Kyle skipped the rest of the movie and simply talked by the fireside, holding hands. A little about her life in California. A little about his growing up on the farm. A lot about their spiritual goals. Had she and Brent ever discussed growing in Christ or serving others? If they did, she couldn't remember sharing her heart, as she had with Kyle. He seemed to enjoy every word she spoke.

By the time he left, she had to fight the urge to kiss him. She detected the same desire in him—or was it the fireplace's embers reflected in those deep, dark eyes? At least he released her hand very reluctantly when they said good night. For they both had agreed that for the boys' sake—and until they knew each other better—they should take this relationship slowly. Carefully. Prayerfully.

What a conversation. What a night.

What a man.

Chapter 11

"Don't set a plate for me, Mom." Kyle stuck his head inside the kitchen door before heading across the field to his house.

Kyle's mother stopped in the middle of mashing potatoes. "But you usually eat Friday night dinner with us. I made pot roast. Your favorite."

His stomach growled at the mouth-watering fragrance of brown gravy bubbling on the stove. "I'm sorry you went to all that trouble. I really appreciate it, Mom, and from now on, I'll let you know ahead of time. But I have plans tonight. And I still need to shower."

"You have plans every night, it seems." She plunged the masher into the pot as if attacking the potatoes. Her nose had turned bright pink. Not a good sign.

"Aren't you the one who wanted me to go out more?" Maybe Mom had had one of those days. He tried to lighten things up. "I've actually learned to talk to somebody besides my horse."

"I wish you'd stuck with horses." She dumped milk into the potatoes.

Whoa. What was up with Mom? He entered and grabbed a spoon. Stirring gravy beside her, he said carefully, "Do you want to explain what you just said?"

"Will it do any good?" Now her nose turned fire engine red. He'd learned long ago that signaled "You're in for it, son."

Her tone grated on him. After all, he was thirty years old, not thirteen. Still, he needed to know what this was all about. Kyle intentionally lowered his voice. "Please tell me why you're upset."

She whipped the gas burner off and clapped a metal lid on the pan. "First, you let Brittany get away—"

"Mom, once and for all, our breakup was a good thing." He could not make her understand that her idea of a soul mate was not his.

She snorted. "That aside, I could name a hundred wonderful girls in this county you could date. But no. You spend every blessed minute with that woman."

"That woman?" He couldn't have felt more floored if she'd dumped the gravy on him. "When did Lauren become 'that woman'? Are you sure we're talking about the same girl? Lauren Pellegrino?"

"Yes." She crossed her arms like swords.

"Mom, you don't even know her—"

"I know all about her."

He choked back an angry denial. Taking a slow breath, he chose his words as if selecting seed. "I was going to ask if I could bring her for dinner soon, so you could become better acquainted."

"Al, tell Kyle why that is not going to happen." She glared at his dad, who had stepped inside. Dad looked as if he wanted to escape.

"Rose, we agreed to discuss this at length with Kyle—not dump it on him as he's going out the door."

"Discuss what?" Now Kyle crossed his arms.

"Be still," a quiet voice whispered. *"Remember what you learned the last time you argued with them."*

He did not want to listen.

Dad turned away from them and poured water into his beloved Mr. Coffee. "Your mother and I are concerned because you've suddenly fallen for someone we don't know, a woman from California." He said the last word as if Lauren hailed from Uzbekistan. "A woman who's been married before, with two children."

He truly loved his parents. But sometimes he wondered if he'd been adopted at birth. "Dad, Lauren's a courageous widow who moved to the Midwest so she could raise her children in a healthy, friendly"—he gritted his teeth— "environment. And she's Hort's niece. Hort Hayworth, a friend you've known all your life."

"Still, a second marriage always brings baggage." Now his mother's eyes held a pleading look. She clutched his arm. "We want you to be happy, Kyle. We want the very best for you."

"I am happy, Mom." He touched her hand. "Lauren and I haven't even mentioned marriage yet. We've barely begun dating. She doesn't want to rush into things—"

"I know you like kids, but think hard before you consider raising somebody else's sons." Dad, still facing the coffeepot, continued as if Kyle hadn't spoken. "Nine generations of Hammonds have farmed our land. Nine." His face stretched tight as leather, Dad faced Kyle. "I don't want to will the farm to boys who are not my blood kin."

"The farm? You think the farm comes first?" Ire billowed through Kyle like a flash fire. "Bottom line, it's just dirt. And dirt is not as important as people." He had to get away. Now. "Mom, Dad, I want to believe you mean well. But I have to go. Good-bye."

He charged out the door, the smell of scorched gravy following him. As a kid ticked with his parents, he'd slammed the screen door. Today, he refrained. Still, their attitude made him wish he could yank it off its hinges.

Lauren had known today was the day, but that didn't mean she felt prepared. If only she could have persuaded the boys to find out about the final cuts tomorrow. Her mother always said any news, good or bad, looked better by daylight.

Logan and Ethan wanted nothing to do with that. They bounced on their beds, off the walls, and off each other until she gave up on threats and bribes and loaded them into her SUV, still clad in pajamas.

Thank heaven the committee chose Friday night for the grand or not-so-grand announcements. They knew kids would stay up late to find out about cuts. Lauren gave thanks those in charge also understood that whether overjoyed or devastated, the children would need to recover before school Monday morning.

"Bet we make all the cuts." Ethan needed more than a seat belt to keep him still. "I like tumbling and the roman ladders. But I want to juggle."

"Me, too." Logan wrestled around, too, but even in the nighttime shadows, she recognized the tense set of his small shoulders.

Uncle Hort, who acted almost as excited as the twins, yanked open the passenger door and jumped into the front seat. "There'll be a bunch of people down at the Center. The trainers post the lists on the wail—the windows out front."

He almost said "wailing wall," the back side of the building where cuts were posted during years past. Uncle Hort rolled his eyes, annoyed with himself.

He'd done too many things right to worry about one almost-slip. Guiding the car with her left hand, Lauren patted his reassuringly. Whatever happened tonight, she could count on his support to help the boys.

Uncle Hort was a true prophet. Many more headlights than

usual shone in downtown Peru—except when the Tigers had won the basketball sectional the previous month. Then half the town stayed up all night. She'd razzed Uncle Hort because he'd caroused with his buddies downtown as if they were sixteen.

Lauren parked, and they hurried to the front of the Center. Children flitted between clumps of parents like manic schools of minnows. Teens draped over cars and each other, trying to assume a "whatever" persona. When dark figures appeared inside the shadowy building, taping up giant pieces of paper, all ages surged forward as one.

"Ethan!" Her son's hand slipped from hers as if her skin were oiled. He pushed his way toward the list labeled Jugglers in big red letters. Logan escaped, too, but the crowd shoved him the wrong direction, away from his goal. With Uncle Hort's help, however, he was gradually making headway. Whom should she follow? Ethan probably would make the juggling cut. He always shone in the athletic department. But would he this time? And Logan…she didn't want to think about his chances. A single mom with twins should be granted some sort of space-and-time dispensation to cope with moments like these.

"The boys didn't go to bed early tonight?" Kyle's teasing voice tickled her ear.

She felt his strong hand on her shoulder, and half the burden of uneasiness lifted. She threw him a smile then edged toward the windows.

"Lauren, you should know—"

She heard the note of warning, but he didn't need to tell her. Ethan was jumping up and down as if he could soar past the streetlights.

Logan, standing before the juggling list, had frozen into a statue. Though he did not face her, she felt the blue blankness of his stare, the immobile set of his mouth. No tears. Not in public. Uncle Hort, bless him, had slipped an arm around

Logan. She stopped. Maybe that was what her son needed right now—another guy who understood how he felt.

"I'm sorry. I wish I could have told you all beforehand. But I have to follow the rules."

She tore her gaze away from her son. Kyle's honest brown eyes searched hers. "I made decisions I thought were best for everybody. Ethan is ready to juggle. Logan isn't."

"I know." She hadn't touched Kyle's cheek before, but now she needed to. Uncle Hort was helping Logan, but she craved comfort, too. She wanted to feel the warmth of this slightly prickly, masculine face that helped calm the gales of emotion slamming her insides.

"Logan did make the roman ladder group. And he'll get to do tumbling, too."

His gentle words calmed her storm. She nodded, thanking God they'd followed Uncle Hort's advice to try out for more than one event. Kyle raised a hand and ran it gently over her fingers. They dropped hands almost immediately, but the invisible ribbon of feeling that tied them together remained as they walked to the windows, where mingled celebration and sorrow reigned.

Chapter 12

Lauren licked a stray string of hot fudge from her fingers then twirled the counter stool an extra turn before she rose to leave the Sunnyside. Now that her hours had returned to normal, she could pick up the boys herself and spend more time watching practices—and Kyle. Her cheeks warmed. Did her face match her new peach top?

"You're looking pretty springy these days." Sylvia handed Lauren her paycheck as she rang up her brownie sundae. She appeared almost as happy to grant Lauren her first substantial raise as Lauren was to receive it. Her boss cast a look around the nearly empty café then gave her a girl-talk look from heavily mascaraed eyes. "Pretty and springy."

"It's gorgeous outside." Lauren hugged herself. "Uncle Hort said when spring finally comes to Indiana, she really outdoes herself." Dogwood trees, with their clouds of pink and white blossoms, adorned the countryside like huge bouquets. Kyle had given her a quick driving tour of his family's fields, with their fresh green stripes of young corn plants and soybeans. "How could I ever think of it as barren and lifeless?"

"It is lovely. But I wouldn't be surprised if this change of perspective has something to do with a certain guy, too."

Lauren laughed and waved good-bye as she left. She'd tried to keep Kyle and her a secret. Such naïveté! The Peru grapevine never slept.

Now she didn't care if the whole county knew. As she almost skipped down the street, a daisy sun smiled at her from a blue-denim sky. *Lord, You always bring spring after winter, don't You? When Brent died, I thought the sun would never shine again. I'm sorry I didn't believe You.*

Arriving at the Circus City Center, she almost balked at going inside. But nothing, not even a glorious day, matched the pleasure of watching her sons—and Kyle. Entering the arena, she shut her eyes and threw her head back, inhaling the scene. Even if no popcorn fragrance greeted her, she would know where she was, sensing the vast barn-like space, its lighted ceiling strung with intricate rigging. The energy of performers practicing, practicing, practicing. Not wanting to miss anything, she opened her eyes. In ring one, several middle and high school boys and girls wearing leotards and shorts balanced on huge, glittery gold and red balls, carefully edging them with their feet into a parade line.

Ethan already had told her about them—"I want to do rolling globes one year, Mom." She sighed. Ethan wanted to try every event. By the time he finished high school, he probably would.

High school? The words shook her, as if she teetered on a globe, too. But the thought that Ethan and Logan could grow up in this close-knit community warmed her even more than the pleasant spring day. After the boys' Skype session last night with her mother-in-law, Lauren felt more thankful than ever that she made the difficult decision to move to Peru.

Why did she camp her thoughts under the one dark little

cloud in her sky? She stuffed the image of Marian and Preston into a mental file and locked it.

Walking toward the bleachers, she shifted her attention to a light-haired, older girl, who was gradually working her ball up a ramp then down a set of steps. Lauren wanted to yell encouragement—"You can do it, hon!" But at this point, she'd only distract the teen. Besides, Lauren's knees still wobbled when she watched any act that might result in a major fall. She turned and hurried past pairs of other older children hanging from large white ladders attached to ceiling cables. Nets and the watchful eyes of trainers and spotters below helped keep the kids safe, but her stomach lurched. The twins did their beginning gymnastic moves on specially adapted roman ladders on the ground. She wouldn't have to hold her breath while her boys dangled high in the air.

She wandered near the center ring, where Logan was practicing his double somersault. She slipped behind a group of other moms talking along the sidelines, not wanting him to know she was watching. Logan curled his thin body into a ball, slowing down and rolling a little sideways as he completed his move. But a host of other children, mostly younger than him, rolled and tumbled like puppies, too, often meandering off the mats. Here Logan could show off a little. Grinning, she heard him yell advice to a first grader.

She spotted Kyle and the jugglers in ring three. Ethan handled three clubs quite well. Last week he'd struggled, often dropping them. But now his movements flowed as smoothly as some of the older boys'. He was even trying a flourish or two. Kyle, standing behind Ethan, coached him as if her son were the only juggler in the world. The care and patience he displayed in his work with the twins—and with all the children—had made a huge difference in their attitudes. Especially Logan's.

She'd expected an asthma meltdown the night of final cuts. Of course Logan cried, once they returned to the SUV. Sniffling as she drove home, she wanted to dissolve in a pool of miserable tears herself. But Kyle dropped by briefly, talking seriously with both her sons as they drank hot chocolate in Uncle Hort's kitchen.

"Logan, I'd like you to keep working as my assistant."

"You would?" A spark of wonder in those sad little eyes. Lauren's puddled over.

"Yes. If you keep watching the jugglers, keep learning, and keep practicing, your chances for making the group next year look good. Will you do it?" Kyle extended his hand.

"Sure!" Logan shook it, a tiny smile tugging at his mouth. They bumped knuckles.

Kyle told Ethan he expected him to aid his brother in reaching his potential. Kyle's man-to-man approach appeared to help both far more than weepy sympathy from her. The fact Logan made the tumbling and roman ladder teams also cheered him. He'd needed his inhaler a little more that weekend, and he spent more time playing alone, but no emergency room visit had materialized.

Now as Lauren watched, Logan, who had just completed his tumbling act, moved to the juggling area. Carrying Kyle's big clipboard with an air of extreme responsibility, he marked attendance. Logan also distributed clubs and Hacky Sacks to the jugglers and served as Kyle's gofer. Today Ethan coached his brother during their session's free time, helping him smooth out his two-club moves. When the group finished, Lauren knew Ethan would even help Logan clean up and pack up.

Wouldn't it be great if they cooperated like this at home? How did Kyle do it?

Demonstrating a trick to three teens, he tossed a club so high it drew her eye to it—and to him. Who would expect such a big man to possess such agile hands? Kyle and the advanced jugglers formed a rectangle, tossing and exchanging clubs so fast Lauren couldn't follow them. Several went flying, and Lauren ducked, though they landed a fair distance from the bleachers.

His eye found hers. She felt as if jumper cables stretched between them. Though she'd felt happy when she'd walked into the circus arena, delicious electricity now sparked every breath she took.

Kyle assigned all the jugglers more exercises and walked toward her. She knew the glow in his dark eyes must match her own.

"Still pretty outside?" Standing beside her, he extended his right index finger toward her hand.

"Lovely." She touched it with her own. "I can't remember a more beautiful day."

"Let's make it even better. Are you up for canoeing this evening?"

"With the twins?" She straightened her shoulders, realizing that the busy workday had taken its toll.

He laughed. "No, let's take them some Saturday when we feel like getting wet." He ran his finger over her hand. "Tonight I'd like to spend a quiet moonlit evening on the Mississinewa Reservoir with you. Just you."

Boldly grasping his hand, she forgot about their audience of kids, trainers, and parents. "I can't think of anything I'd rather do."

"I see everyone's making excellent progress, Kyle." Julie's voice broke in. Mischief sizzled in her eyes.

Lauren jumped, dropping his hand. Sometimes she felt like she and Kyle starred on a giant 1960s drive-in movie screen watched by the entire town: *California Girl Meets Corn King.*

"Sorry." Her friend drained the tease from her tone. "I grew up with a 24-7 small-town audience. Sometimes I forget you didn't."

"It—it takes a little getting used to." Lauren's smile escaped. "In LA, nobody found me interesting. Blah, actually."

"Can you believe that?" Kyle looked at her as if she'd just declared the earth was flat.

"Well, we think you're awesome." Julie threw her arm around Lauren's shoulders.

Maddy, sitting in her stroller, clapped her hands. "Yay!"

"See. It's unanimous." Kyle grabbed her hand again.

Lauren felt the see-all, know-all Peru camera zoom in for a close-up, but with the look Kyle gave her, she didn't care.

Julie picked up the baby, who grabbed a handful of her mother's face. Julie spoke through the sweet torture, not missing a beat. "Actually, I was going to ask if your twins could come with us to the park for a fast-food picnic after practice. It's way too pretty to eat inside."

"What, you need more excitement in your life?" Juggling five clubs at once sounded easier than juggling five children.

"Ben will help when he gets off work." Julie shrugged. "Besides, Matt would love having *two* other boys around. For once, he won't feel outnumbered by his sisters."

"I'll pick up subs for everybody and drop them by with the boys." Lauren knew her bonus wouldn't buy the moon, but what fun to treat someone else! "Maconaquah Park, right?"

"Yep. Down at the shelter past the school, near the playground." Maddy was still twisting Julie's mouth like a red licorice stick. "Don't worry about what kind of subs to buy. My kids eat my cooking. They'll eat anything."

"Are you sure you don't need me?"

"Nope. Some other time." Julie pushed the stroller away before Lauren could object. "You have important things to do."

Like spending a whole evening with Kyle? Alone? Her feelings lit up like a Hollywood marquee on Oscar night.

But Kyle dropped her hand. He shook his head. Her excitement died as if he'd pulled a plug.

"I don't know." He clicked his tongue. "We'd have to eat dinner together, too." He lowered his voice. "All—by—ourselves."

She tried to keep her voice casual. "Do you think we can handle that?"

He bent his head so close she could hear him breathe. He murmured into her ear, "I'd like to try."

"I didn't know you owned a canoe." Lauren, carrying the bow to the beach, tried to act as if it didn't weigh her down.

"I've canoed on both the Mississinewa Reservoir and River since I was a Cub Scout." He grinned. "You'll be glad to know I steer much better now than then."

He'd wanted to carry the canoe to the launch alone, but she would have none of it. Her slim shoulders refused to bow as she strained to keep her load from touching the ground. The last strong rays of early evening found her hair, highlighting each strand as if they had discovered gold.

Kyle and Lauren reached the shoreline and dumped the canoe. He surveyed the reservoir's wide sheet of rippling emerald water, estimating how much daylight they had left.

"Beautiful." Lauren threw her hands open wide as if to give the world a hug. "I had no idea Indiana could look like a movie set."

"It is pretty, isn't it." He'd never seen her this relaxed— fresh as new leaves, her face flushed pink as the dogwoods clustered near the boat landing. For once, he wished he owned a rowboat instead. They could row sitting side by side. He handed her a life jacket and watched her strap it on, envying its closeness to her. "You're not afraid of the water, are you?"

"No." She gave him a quizzical grin, her eyebrows arched in a "Why do you ask?"

A little late for that question. But at circus practice, she'd acted as if she feared heights, bumps—anything that might threaten her boys. Maybe it was just a mom thing. He shrugged then helped her into the canoe, preparing to shove off.

They glided out into the lake. Most motorized boats out tonight were manned by fishing addicts intent on their lines and bobbers. He liked kids—especially hers—but he didn't mind that their spectators this evening consisted mostly of turtles on their log front porches and blue herons. The tall wading birds stared at them with almost parental disapproval then flew off, long legs dangling behind them.

Maybe the canoe worked out better after all, because he played spectator without Lauren's knowing it. Her slender silhouette swayed and bent as she paddled forward into a sky that looked like God set a field of roses on fire. Eventually he realized she didn't slap her paddle on the water or flap it around. Instead, her long, sleek strokes told him she not only had done this before but had received some advanced training. "Who taught you how to paddle a canoe?"

"I was a camp counselor for several summers during high school." She paused midstroke, not turning to look at him. "Brent—my late husband—was my instructor."

A cord of jealousy spiraled through him. *Hammond, cool it. You knew she was married before.*

Her head dipped, and her shoulders, so straight and strong, wilted.

Great move. A perfect evening, and you had to ruin it. Breaking the awkward silence, he said, "I'm sorry I stirred up sad memories."

A small, forgiving smile over her shoulder. "You didn't know." She dipped her paddle into the water again. "Maybe we'll talk about him sometime. But if you don't mind, I'd just like to enjoy this gorgeous evening with you."

"Works for me." Relief coursed through him. A full moon barely peeked over the horizon. The spring breeze whispered of even better things to come.

With the darkening sky, they paddled back to the landing. He jumped out of the canoe and pushed it up on the sand. She grabbed the paddles.

"I'll load this thing up." He tugged it completely out of the water then paused, his heart beating in fast, syncopated rhythm. "If you'd like, we can drive to the beach. I know a great spot where we can watch the moon rise."

"It really is too lovely to go home."

Actually, who needed the moon? Her face lit up the night.

The beach hadn't opened for swimmers yet. They parked Kyle's camp chairs under the trees behind the peaceful expanse of sand and water. Simultaneously, they reached for each other's hands.

Was there such a thing as a camp love seat? If there was, Kyle would buy one before their next trip to Mississinewa. But tonight they sat close together, holding hands and listening to the frog chorus and other night creatures warbling their spring love songs. Sometimes talking. Mostly listening and enjoying.

Many women he'd known would have tried to stuff the quiet with words. Lauren knew how to enjoy silence for itself.

When she finally exclaimed at the late hour and they rose to leave, he reached for her, and she came to him in a kiss so tender, so soul shaking, that he knew he wouldn't sleep for hours. They shared another kiss on Hort's front porch when they said a sweet, aching good night, and a hundred dreams for the future filled his cup of joy to overflowing.

Later, however, as Kyle sat wide-awake on his deck, the glare of the security lights surrounding his parents' nearby house and barn dispelled his reverie. Their pesky voices buzzed in his ear like gnats out of reach.

"A second marriage always brings baggage."

Possibly true, he thought. *But maybe I'm the guy who can help her carry it for a while—then help her lose it.*

Chapter 13

Tucked back in a corner of the Sunnyside kitchen, Lauren's desk boasted a small vase with three red tulips—enough colorful joy to keep her smiling all day. Kyle must have come when Sylvia first arrived, at the crack of dawn, when Lauren was still trying to help Ethan find his math homework and left tennis shoe. How could Kyle have risen so early when they'd stayed at the reservoir so late?

I wish I could have seen him before he left. But on reading the accompanying note, she heard his voice again:

> *This year, my tulips bloomed for the first time— just for you! Come see more at my house Sunday after church. Bring the boys, and we'll have the first barbecue of the year.*
>
> *Yours,*
> *Kyle*

P.S. Make sure they're hungry.

The "yours" sent a delicious shiver up her spine. What a special evening they'd spent together at Mississinewa. She hadn't been kissed like that in years.

Maybe never.

And now an invitation to his house with the boys. It sounded so family-ish—to her. Did it to him?

A blast of cold air from the walk-in brought her back to Sunnyside. Lauren shook herself, trying to dispel the romantic fog. That's what came of floating around in a canoe with a handsome guy under starry skies. She'd done that before—

"Pretty flowers." Sylvia, bustling past with an armload of lettuce, paused. "Why the frown? Aren't they from you-know-who?"

"Yes, they're from Kyle." Lauren let herself grin. "As if you didn't know."

"That's better." Sylvia shook a finger at her. "A girl with all the reason in the world to smile *should*."

"I just want to be careful. For the boys' sake." Lauren took several heads from her, hauled out the big salad bin, and after donning gloves, began to tear lettuce for lunch.

"I've known Kyle since he was in diapers, and you can trust me on this, hon." Sylvia dumped the rest on a nearby table and stuck her hands on her ample hips. "If you're looking for someone to love you and your boys, you couldn't do better if you ordered a man custom-designed."

"Probably not many like him on the internet," Lauren deadpanned.

Her boss *humphed*. "Nor anywhere else." To Lauren's surprise, Sylvia cupped her face in chilly hands. "Don't be afraid to be happy, hon. Life's too short to waste precious time looking for problems that don't exist."

Her eyes moist, Sylvia patted Lauren's cheeks. "I'll fetch the carrots and tomatoes." She turned and hurried into the walk-in.

Lauren turned back to salad-making, but the woman's

words percolated inside her. *She's still in love with Roy, though he's gone. How she must miss him.*

Did she miss Brent like that? Not so much. Especially lately. She stopped shredding, removing a glove to touch one of the tulips' soft, scarlet petals, peering inside at its golden heart. Maybe it really was time to tell Brent good-bye.

And to welcome a new love with wide-open arms?

"Man, does that smell good!" Ethan and Logan sniffed the air hungrily. They started to charge around Kyle's nice-but-not-so-neat brick ranch, but Lauren reminded them, "We're guests, guys. Stay here at the front door with me. Logan, please ring the doorbell."

A joyous, untidy bed of red tulips under the front windows reminded her of Kyle's romantic surprise a few days before. She tried to calm her thoughts and stomach as the tangy, to-matoey fragrance drifted past.

"Hey." Kyle stuck his head around the corner of the house. "I should have told you to come around back."

"Hi." His delighted grin reenergized her butterflies.

Logan rolled his eyes. "Now can we go to the backyard?"

"Sure."

The boys dashed around the corner, Lauren following at her usual slow jog. Reaching both hands toward hers, Kyle met her. "Welcome to my house."

She tried to shake off the near-hypnosis his eyes induced. "You should have let me bring something."

"And miss the chance to show off my cooking?" His arm slipped around her shoulders as they followed the boys. "Some of my family members have won awards for our secret bar-becue sauce. And thanks to my mom, I make a mean potato salad. You'll want to come back and see me again." His bi-ceps tightened. "And again. And again—"

"Way cool! Hey, Mom!"

The twins' yell came almost as a relief. She sped up her pace, Kyle easily matching her steps.

"Come see the statues." Logan crossed Kyle's fuzzy-white-dandelion-filled backyard, pointing at an odd assortment of whimsical-looking objects and creatures, all carved of wood.

Lauren bent down to run her fingers over the smooth head of a boxy-looking bear.

"That was my first attempt, when I was in high school. I like my circus stuff best." He pointed to a grouping of five juggling clubs, a miniature circus wagon, and an amazing six-foot, totem-pole-like carving in the corner. Its clown faces, happy and sad, looked almost alive.

"That's my most recent one. Took me forever, but I like it."

His obvious talent blew her away. "How did you do all this?"

"Did you use lots of knives?" At Ethan's eager question, she couldn't repress a small shudder.

"Nope. Mostly chain saws." Kyle glanced at his watch. "I'd better go check on our chicken and ribs, or we'll need one to cut them."

The boys dogged his heels as he strode to a wooden deck and its big stainless steel grill. Lauren followed slowly. What else didn't she know about this man?

"Just about ready." Kyle lowered the fire beneath the meat and closed the grill lid. He opened the french doors to the kitchen and pointed at a comfortable-looking, tan patio chair near a picnic table. "Lauren, please have a seat and enjoy the view. You guys want to give me a hand with the rest of dinner?"

"Yeah, I'm starved!" Ethan's helpfulness increased dramatically when food was involved.

"I'll be glad to set the table—"

"With three able-bodied guys like us to do the work? No way." He gestured to the twins. "Your mom works in a restaurant all the time. We want her to relax and enjoy herself, don't we?"

"Yeah!" They trailed after Kyle.

Well, why not? She plopped into the patio chair and surveyed Kyle's kingdom. No flowers other than the dandelions here. Besides big maples shading the deck, a scraggly but pretty apple tree waved branches covered with creamy blossoms. Its sweet undercurrent of fragrance blended with the spicy barbecue smells. She heard the gurgle of a small stream somewhere—maybe concealed in those trees behind the back fence. The ever-present fields bordered the other two sides—fields striped with little corn and soybean plants, eager and growing as children in a schoolyard.

And the wonderful wood carvings. Even from here, she felt Kyle's investment of himself in them. The chain saw aspect bothered her, though. If only he preferred painting—

The french doors flew open, and a trio of smiling servers carried paper plates, plastic silverware, and food to the picnic table. Kyle lit an orange citron candle with a flourish then headed for the grill with a large platter. "Dinner is served."

Ethan volunteered to say grace, which surprised her, as Logan usually did the honors.

"God, thank You for all this yummy food. And thanks that Mr. Hammond's our friend and lets us come to his house. Amen."

"I'm glad you're my friends, too." Sitting across from Lauren, he locked his gaze on her. "Is it okay if they call me Kyle?"

Most of the kids did. But Lauren could see it wasn't a casual question.

She paused then returned his intensity. "Yes, that's fine."

More silence. She couldn't tear her eyes from him. Why did she feel as if they'd just said something monumental? It wasn't like he'd proposed marriage—

"Um, Kyle?"

"Yes, Ethan?"

"Can we eat?"

Laughing, Kyle ruffled his hair. Giggles bubbled out of Lauren's nose like ginger ale. Kids were good for a romance. They brought you back to planet earth.

Still grinning, Kyle poised his tongs. "Chicken or ribs, Ethan? Or a little of both?"

"Both."

"Me, too." Logan's hungry eyes gleamed.

Lauren served the twins and filled her own plate. Kyle was right about his "mean" potato salad. The chicken and ribs, juicy, yet crispy and blackened outside, had been cooked by a master chef. She used a half-dozen paper napkins to swipe away sauce from her cheeks and fingers, but knew she must look as sticky as her sons.

"That was absolutely delicious." She'd thought he'd cooked far too much meat, but they finished off all but a couple of ribs and one chicken leg.

"Breakfast tomorrow." Kyle gave her a wicked grin.

She ignored the boys' envious glances. "Your mother wouldn't like that, I'll bet."

To her surprise, his smile faded. "No, she wouldn't. But I'm a big boy now." He gathered paper plates. "Ready for dessert?"

"Ooh, I don't think I could eat another bite."

Of course, the twins thought otherwise. "I can."

"Me, too!"

Kyle's grin returned. "Let's wash up then take a little walk together. We'll go see Baby Jewel before we eat strawberry shortcake."

"Baby Jewel?" Logan's eyes scrunched into slits. "Why are we going to see a baby?"

"A baby horse. A filly. Her name is Jewel, but we call her "Baby" because she's only a few months old."

"Can we pet her?"

"Maybe. Her mother doesn't know you, and we'll have to

see how she feels about it today." He smiled at Lauren. "Moms are kind of careful about who touches their babies."

After a quick cleanup, Kyle led them through a back fence gate to the woods bordering his yard. Sure enough, a small, clear stream wound through the trees, complaining noisily about rocks and tree roots blocking its way.

"Let's wade!" Ethan yanked off his shoes before Lauren could stop him.

"Hey, that's why God made creeks." When Kyle pulled his off, too, Logan followed suit.

She retrieved the boys' shoes and tied their shoestrings together. Kyle took them while she slipped out of her Crocs and rolled up her jeans. "Ooh. You would think this water would have warmed up by now."

"It has out in the pastures, where the sun hits the water. Not necessarily in the woods." Kyle's hand closed over hers, and they wandered behind the boys as they threw pebbles and chased minnows.

What would it be like to spend every Sunday afternoon with this man?

Her wary side waggled a cautious finger. *Too much! Too fast!*

"Don't be afraid to be happy." Sylvia's words called to her. *Lord, how do I handle this?*

She hadn't planned to fall in love again.

What do I do?

She'd fallen for Brent, but he'd fallen off a mountain. Falling always led to a good-bye.

Amid her swirling thoughts, the quiet, no-nonsense voice spoke. *"Trust Me."*

Giant oaks and sycamores along the stream bent protectively over the boys as they played, whispering prayers only God could understand. Lauren breathed the earthy fragrance of the forest, created by decades of rain, snow, and sun. Chat-

tery sparrows, busy robins, and brilliant cardinals all sang a
Sunday afternoon hymn to the One who cared for them.

Could He not care for her, too? For her sons? For Kyle?

"You're quiet." Kyle's words held an unasked question.

"Just thinking. And praying a little." She searched the tran-
quil forest before them. Too peaceful. With the twins, quiet
usually meant trouble. "Where are the boys?"

He chuckled. "Just ran around that big rock on the left.
Headed where I want them to go, though they don't know it."

How did he *do* that? Her sons, like curious puppies on
leashes, often had to be dragged toward the correct desti-
nation.

He called, "Hey, guys, let's go check out the horses. Wait
for your mom and me near that big metal gate."

Kyle pulled her along, his long legs eating up ground.
"Want me to carry you?"

Kyle's offer sounded way too good—for several reasons.
"No, I'll make it." Panting, she spotted the twins zooming
through the stream like amphibious vehicles. Sharp bits of
gravel jabbed her feet. Did the boys run so fast their feet
only skimmed them? Her sons, both wearing mantles of mud
and greeny goo, rattled the gate, turning to watch the slower
grown-ups.

Kyle enclosed her waist with his hands, sailing her over
the final stretch of pebbly, muddy creek bed to the soft grass
beyond. She felt lithe and lovely, like a ballerina who need
never return to earth.

Kyle unlocked the padlock while they all donned their
shoes. "Hey, Ruby," he called across the sunny, clover-dotted
pasture before them. He gave a sharp whistle. "Come here,
girl. You, too, Baby Jewel."

"Oh"—Lauren stopped in her tracks—"they're—they're
beautiful, Kyle."

A glossy chestnut mare, swishing her thick tail, walked
cautiously toward them, an almost-black filly trailing behind

her. Not that Lauren knew anything about horses, but she'd never seen one that color. With the sun shining on the filly's coat, iridescent tints of red glimmered all over her. No wonder Kyle named her Jewel.

He quickly placed himself between the horses and the boys, who were making a beeline straight for the animals. "Whoa, guys. Let me see what kind of mood Ruby's in before you approach her. We want her to stay happy, and we want you to stay safe. Stand here with your mom."

She liked his firmness. Ethan and Logan stopped their headlong dash. The mare neighed and shook her mane, but quieted as Kyle petted her, talking to her in a low, soothing tone and feeding her carrots from his pockets. Baby Jewel, eyes gleaming with curiosity, wandered a few steps toward Lauren and the twins. She cautioned, "Don't move. Not until Kyle tells you."

"That's right." He left Ruby and walked back to Lauren and the twins, pulling apple slices from his pockets. "I saved these for you because Ruby likes them best. You need to let her know you're friendly before she will let you touch her baby."

"Now walk with me slowly, guys. Never make sudden moves, especially if an animal doesn't know you." He glanced at Lauren. "I brought plenty of apples. Care to join us?"

"I'll just watch this time." Too late, she realized he might equate her reluctance with fear of horses. In reality she wanted to watch *him*—with her boys. Maybe next time—oh, how she hoped there would be a next time!—she would make the horses' acquaintance up close and personal. Right now, her eyes followed Kyle's athletic, blue-jeaned figure across the pasture. Lauren grinned as Ethan and Logan tried to imitate Kyle, step for step, as they approached the mare.

Their efforts paid off. Not only did Ruby welcome the apples and the boys' gentle pats, she did not flinch when Kyle introduced Logan and Ethan to Baby Jewel.

After a few minutes, Kyle took the boys' hands. "Okay,

that's enough for the first visit. We'll pet the horses longer next time."

Lauren's heart sang as they took a more direct way back to Kyle's home along an unused gravel road. She almost wished her sons would maintain their usual twenty-foot head start. Now, tired somewhat by the hike, they hovered well within earshot. She and Kyle had to restrain their conversation to chitchat. Still, the sweet pressure of Kyle's fingers on hers and his potent glances told her what she wanted to hear.

As they broke through the forest, however, Kyle stopped so suddenly she stumbled. His warm fingers around hers turned rigid.

"Did we misunderstand, Kyle?" His mother, still dressed in her Sunday best, stood on the deck in front of the French doors, frowning. "We thought you wanted us to stop by for dessert."

Chapter 14

"Hi, Mom." Kyle forced himself to sound cordial. "I thought you said you couldn't come."

At the sight of his mother, the boys had scuttled back to Lauren like chicks to a hen. She was smiling, but he read all kinds of question marks in her eyes.

"We put the coffeepot on, son," Dad boomed from inside the kitchen.

"Thanks." Kyle didn't want to say it because he'd asked them a hundred times not to enter his house without permission. Somehow he had to salvage this important encounter between his folks and Lauren and the twins. Still holding her hand, he led them up the steps to the deck. "Mom, Dad, I'm sure you remember meeting Hort's niece Lauren, and her boys, Ethan and Logan, when they first came to church."

He put a little emphasis on Hort's name. And *church*.

"Hello, Mr. and Mrs. Hammond."

How could Mom resist that beautiful grin? That soft, lady-like voice?

His mother said nothing. Kyle felt as if he could trip over the hard silence. Lauren's fingers began to pull away from his, but he refused to let go.

His dad wandered out. "Met you back in February, right?"

Lauren brightened. "Yes, in the parking lot, when it was still cold. I had no idea then Indiana could be so beautiful."

"You are from California, aren't you?"

Kyle groaned inwardly. Not a promising direction for the conversation. "Let's all go inside"—*because Mom hates bugs*—"and I'll fix us the best strawberry shortcake in the world. Next to Mom's, of course."

"You're buttering me up." His mother made her *pshaw* sound, but the tight lines around her mouth relaxed somewhat.

"Yay!" The boys, who had been running around the deck like wild ponies, dashed for the doors.

Lauren dropped Kyle's hand and grabbed them by their T-shirts. "First, do you have a garden hose outside? We'd better wash before we enter your house—"

"Good idea." Mom, blocking the doors, eyed Logan and Ethan as if they had arisen from primordial slime.

Though Kyle no longer held Lauren's hand, he felt her stiffen as if she'd turned to steel.

"Over there, around the corner. We could all use a good scrub."

And a breather. He usually shucked his smelly barnyard clothes in his utility room—and often did it in his parents' mudroom, without a word of protest from Mom. But now he only reached inside the nearby door and pulled old towels from the cabinet while Lauren corralled the boys. Trying to kid them about who was the grossest, he led them to the faucet, blessing the excuse to put some distance between them and his mother.

Otherwise he might say something that would make an incredible mess of everything—one that never could be cleaned up.

* * *

Logan aimed the hose at Ethan, who tried to wrestle it away.

"Stop it, boys!" Actually, Lauren felt tempted to let them turn the washing session into an all-out water war. Then she could make her excuses, snatch her kids up, and take them home to Uncle Hort and his love-filled cookie jar—far away from Mrs. Hammond's critical eyes. During their brief encounter at church, she'd remembered his parents as friendly, like the other church people. They'd only exchanged a few "hellos" in passing since then, so why the coldness?

Kyle sprayed Ethan's hands and arms then started on Logan while she dabbed at Ethan's muddy face.

"I'm not a little kid, Mom. I can wash my own face." He sloshed the washcloth across his cheeks, spreading the dirt like glaze on a cupcake. Logan did the same.

Right. "Okay, you two wash first. Then I'll see if you need a touch-up."

Kyle started his own cleanup while Lauren scrubbed her hands and face. Running her fingers through her hair, she brushed leaves and who knows what else from its stringy strands. Her mud-spattered jeans looked almost as bad as the twins'. If only they could leave.

"Please stay." Kyle's low voice in her ear told her he'd been reading her thoughts.

Despite her imploding mood, his nearness struck the usual spark of longing in her. Matching his tone, she said, "I'm not sure it's a good day for this. Maybe we'd better go."

"Aren't we gonna eat strawberry shortcake?"

Logan's hearing was better than the Labs'.

"Why are we washing up if we don't get to eat?" Ethan threw his towel on the ground. "I thought you said—"

"All right." Despite Kyle's mother's hot temper or hot flashes or whatever, Lauren couldn't undermine a near promise.

As the twins cheered, Kyle encircled her waist and whispered, "It will get better. After we eat dessert, the boys and I will juggle. My folks love the circus stuff. You'll see."

"That was delicious, son." Mom, who made a token protest when he loaded her plate, had mellowed. She really did like to eat.

"Your recipe, though it doesn't have your magic touch." Finally Kyle breathed more easily. Maybe his mother would act more civilized now. As long as Dad had his coffee, nuked to boiling, he wouldn't make waves. At least not in front of Lauren and her boys.

"That was *good*." Ethan and Logan, having finished off second helpings, no longer fidgeted in their chairs.

"It was wonderful, Kyle." Lauren's smile warmed him all over. "Sorry I couldn't quite finish it—"

"Mom never finishes her peach pie at Sunnyside either, even though there's nothing wrong with it." Logan's tone implied he'd never understand the mystery of mothers.

"She's always on a diet," Ethan scoffed. "She says she has to stay thin." He aimed his gaze at Kyle's mother's empty dish. "But it's okay if you eat all your dessert, Mrs. Hammond. Old ladies are supposed to get fat."

They all sat stunned, as if Ethan had thrown a grenade onto the table.

"Time for our juggling show!" Kyle jumped up, stacking plates. "Head outside, guys. Warm up with the clubs in that big box on the deck. We'll show them our stuff—the best juggling performance in the world, absolutely free!"

His father was pressing his lips together, trying not to grin. At least Dad thought Ethan's comment was funny.

Kyle didn't have to look at either woman to know her feelings on the matter.

"I—I'm sorry." Lauren murmured, slipping from her chair. "I'll go outside and talk to Ethan."

Head bowed, her hair fell forward on her flaming cheeks

as she left. Kyle didn't like the way her shoulders drooped, weighed down as if she were responsible for every uncombed hair on her sons' heads.

"Ethan's just a little kid." He poured Mom another cup then sat down and gave her a gentle poke with his elbow. "Don't you remember the stuff I said when I was his age? Once, after church, I asked you what circumcision was—at Great-aunt Lily's birthday party."

She didn't crack a smile. "You may have been curious, but you were never rude."

He wanted to retort that her memory was failing, but that would only make things worse. "Come on, bring your coffee out on the deck, and I'll show you my new juggling trick. You haven't seen this one."

"I want to see it, too." Dad wasn't always helpful in handling Mom, but this evening, Kyle blessed him.

"All right." His mother rose. "But keep it short. I have a splitting headache."

Funny thing—so did Kyle. But he breathed a silent "*Help me, God!*" and gave her his best smile. "Don't touch the dishes. I'll take care of them later. There's Tylenol in my medicine cabinet. Take a couple then join us outside, okay?" He hugged her, though he didn't feel like it, and walked toward the french doors, trying to think of what he'd say to Lauren.

He needn't have worried.

No droop of Lauren's shoulders now. "Ethan would like to apologize to Mrs. Hammond."

Ethan, of course, looked less than thrilled. But Lauren marched him past Kyle, encountering his parents as they entered the deck.

"Mrs. Hammond, I'm very sorry I hurt your feelings." Ethan's sing-songy apology betrayed Lauren's coaching.

Kyle held his breath. Surely his mom would melt at this little guy's effort to make it right!

At least she nodded and said, "Thank you. I know you didn't mean to."

At the stay of execution, his freckled face lit up. He patted her arm and said, "You're not really that fat."

Lauren's hand went to her forehead as Ethan turned and dashed back to his brother, who was focusing fiercely on juggling two clubs. She dropped into a chair while Mom moved to the opposite side of the deck. Dad shrugged and followed her.

So much for keeping everybody happy. Kyle followed Ethan. The boy had blown the evening away with his way-too-honest comments, but that was one reason Kyle liked kids. Honest. Uncomplicated. And right now, he really needed uncomplicated.

He surveyed Logan's technique. "Keep your eyes on the clubs. Good job. You've got it down."

Logan's serious face broke into a smile. Basking in the boy's satisfaction, Kyle told him to try three.

Ethan, elated at his supposed diplomatic success, juggled three clubs with even more than his usual flair. He tossed several flourishes into the air, catching them effortlessly.

"Pretty good." Dad was trying to hide the fact he was impressed.

"And they're two years younger than I was as a beginner." Maybe things were looking up. At least Lauren and Mom were gazing at the show instead of glaring at each other. For about thirty seconds, Logan managed to juggle three clubs and Ethan dazzled them with a behind-the-back move.

"Ta-da!" Kyle yelled, throwing out his hand to acknowledge them. The boys bowed, as he'd taught them.

He and Lauren clapped the loudest, but his parents joined in polite applause. He bumped knuckles with the twins and sent them to sit with Lauren.

"Now show us your tricks, Kyle!" Logan begged.

Ethan pumped his fist. "Yeah! The ones you said you would do for us today."

"Okay. Just a moment." He unlocked a special section of the equipment box and removed red and yellow clubs, as well as a long, thin case. He stood as far away from the deck and its shade maples as he could while staying within sight of his spectators. The sun was dipping below the trees bordering his yard, leaving just enough daylight for the first part of his act. His heartbeat sped up at the thought of impressing Lauren. She and his parents might actually agree on something, with a little postshow conversation to give this difficult day a positive end. And maybe, after she took the boys home and put them to bed, they could decompress, spending special time together in the swing on Hort's front porch.

"Ladies and gentlemen," he intoned, "I ask that for your safety, you remain in your seats during this dramatic demonstration, unmatched by any juggler in the world." He grinned. "Or in Peru, Indiana."

He opened the case and flipped one machete up—then a second—then two more, never breaking rhythm as he juggled the short, curved swords. He tossed them high into the air and passed them under his legs, twirling them into patterns that slashed the last gaudy pink and gold rays of the sun into ribbons of gleaming color.

A roar of approval from the deck greeted his efforts as he caught the machetes the final time and took a deep bow.

Pulling a lighter from his pocket, he lit five clubs. Hungry flames licked at them as he tossed them into the air. Increasing the tempo, he juggled, pacing back and forth, throwing them faster and faster, until they resembled a wheel of fire. He pitched them high, high, higher into the air, watching them fall, trailing fiery tails like comets, into his hands.

He also loved the high wire, the rush of adrenaline that still flooded him during practice demonstrations as he balanced himself—and another person on his shoulders—while riding a bicycle far above the floor. But the perfect timing and coordination to do these juggling tricks challenged him on every level. The terrible beauty of passing fire and keen, glinting steel through his fingers satisfied something deep and daring inside him.

When he finished with moves that sent the clubs shooting like fireworks above him, his parents' cheers and the twins' shrieks filled him with the joy of success.

Until he realized Lauren's voice had not joined them.

When the others crowded around him with hugs, backslaps, and high fives, she remained silent, back in the dark corner of the deck. When his father flipped on the outside light, Kyle saw her face—eyes big and empty as dark moons, her mouth set as if he'd broken a promise.

Chapter 15

"Are the boys sick?" Uncle Hort, who arrived home late after working in the fields, stared at Lauren. "They didn't go to practice? They seemed fine this morning."

"They were worn out after such a big day yesterday. We came home later than I'd planned." She fixed her eyes on the microwave's timer as she warmed his meal, trying not to remember her hasty departure from Kyle's house, the puzzled pain in his eyes. "I could hardly drag Logan out of bed for school."

"I thought that was pretty normal." Uncle Hort's tone sounded casual, but his sentences all ended in question marks.

She forced herself to chuckle as she brought his plate. "It is, but I think all these circus practices every night are too draining. I don't want the boys' schoolwork to suffer, especially at the end of the year. I think it's best for them to stay home a night or two." Thank heaven, the dryer buzzed. She could end the discussion—for now.

She'd never considered the laundry room a refuge, but tonight, she felt a rush of gratitude that she could shut its door and hide from Uncle Hort's probing and the boys' sullen faces. Even Twinkie and Dinky flopped on her feet, their accusing glares far too much like their young masters'.

She dug through jeans, T-shirts, and at least 103 little socks—an odd number, of course. Why did she bother to fold their clothes? The twins stuffed them into their drawers, wadding them like wastepaper. Still, the repetitive match-the-sleeves, line-up-the-seams routine eased the sandpaper feeling in her stomach.

God, the boys are getting carried away with this circus stuff. They don't realize I'm trying to protect them. For the first time all day, she released the scalding tears in her eyes and heart. *But nobody ever said moms would be popular, right?*

So many times, she'd had to protect her sons from Brent's devil-may-care attitude, counteract the recklessness and irresponsibility that his Hollywood job fostered.

The cell in her pocket vibrated again. She checked it. Six messages, all from Kyle. She turned off her cell. She had left him a message. That was enough.

She'd thought Kyle was different. Who wouldn't—a big, wholesome farmer raised amid the cornfields in Indiana? But like Brent, he lost himself in the rush danger gave him. She'd seen the look on his face as he threw swords, the flames raging in his eyes as he embraced fire—against the blackness of the night, he looked as if he and the inferno were one.

She wouldn't expose her sons to that again.

Besides, she didn't need another mother-in-law from Hades. *I don't need any of this.*

After he heard Lauren's terse message informing him the boys would not return to the circus, Kyle called both Lauren's cell and Hort's landline. Lauren didn't answer and told Hort she couldn't come to the phone. Kyle stopped by the house twice, using the twins' absence as an official excuse. The kids threw their arms around him, and he realized how much he'd missed them, even after only a few days. But Lauren escaped him both times.

So today he would corner her at work after the lunch hour. He wouldn't leave until she talked to him.

Kyle strode across Broadway toward Sunnyside, pausing on the sidewalk to send up a "Help!" prayer. *I don't know what else to do, Father. Please, we need to communicate.*

Lauren was kneeling behind the counter, facing the wall, attaching soft-drink hoses to a fresh carbonation tank. With a mighty grunt, she tried to lift it.

"Want some help with that?"

Her shoulders flinched. "I can do it myself, thank you."

She yanked and yanked on the thing. He looked away, forcing himself to stay seated on the stool. Finally she managed to shove it into the cabinet.

She straightened, her face perspiring. "I'll send Tess to take your order."

"No, Lauren. I don't want Tess to take my order." He leaned across the counter. "I came to talk to you."

Her eyes flashed. "I'm at work, Kyle. This is not an appropriate place to discuss—"

"I've tried lining up an appropriate place. I'm all about appropriate. But you aren't. So I had to come here." He hadn't meant to open the discussion that way, but saying it felt good.

Other women turned red when they were embarrassed or angry. Lauren's cheeks turned peach—one of the things he loved about her.

"All right. I should have explained more about removing the boys from the circus." She raised her eyes then her chin. "I—I just think they're getting obsessed with it. Logan's worn down, the asthma attacks start when he tires. Plus, I want the twins to focus on their schoolwork, not the circus."

"Strange that you haven't mentioned these concerns over the past months."

He was wrong. She did turn red.

"Look, if you don't understand my reasoning, I'm sorry. But a parent has to do the right thing—"

"Why did this 'right thing' magically appear as of last Sunday? Maybe you're just mad at my mother?"

Too blunt. Too loud. Heads bent over afternoon coffee, and newspapers popped up like error messages on computer screens. Lauren, eyes blazing, turned to escape through the kitchen door. But it swung open, Sylvia blocking her way.

"Hello, Kyle." Cheery as ever. "How's the circus going?"

Lauren headed to the opposite end of the counter.

Sylvia halted her with a hand and lowered her voice. "No, dear. You and Kyle need to have a nice cup of coffee together."

Lauren's jaw dropped.

He'd never seen her turn purple. "Sylvia, maybe we'd better do this later—"

"No, now." She turned to Lauren, her voice pleasant, yet crisp. "I'm speaking as your employer. Your disagreement is obviously affecting your work." She gestured to Kyle. "I do not want him loitering at my counter, trying to get your attention." She pointed toward the door. "You're done for the day, Lauren. Paid personal time. Go work it out."

Silence. Then Lauren muttered, "As if we could have a private conversation anywhere in this town."

"Go to Mississinewa." Sylvia smiled. "It's a lovely day—"

Kyle shook his head, even as Lauren blanched. Not Mississinewa. Not his favorite spot, the scene of their first kiss.

"I don't have time to go anywhere. I'm picking up the boys in an hour." Lauren looked at her hands, her feet. Anywhere but at him.

"I'd offer you my office, but I have a conference call in fifteen minutes," Sylvia said. "Use the walk-in. When Roy and I needed a good truth-telling session, we went there. Private. Soundproof."

She moved aside and stuck out a manicured, orange-fingernailed hand. "Go."

Lauren paused then moved forward. Kyle trailed after her, feeling as if he'd been sent to the principal's office. The one time in grade school he'd been caught fighting, he'd prayed all the way to Mr. Keaton's office. Nonstop prayer sure couldn't hurt him now.

The walk-in was chock full of chickens. Sylvia occasionally catered events, and later she would transform the birds into her famous orange-glazed entrée. Somehow the presence of tray after tray of them, plucked, ungainly, and defenseless, embarrassed Lauren. Maybe because she felt almost as helpless.

Or maybe because I'm arguing with a man inside a stupid refrigerator.

Kyle cleared his throat. Again. She hadn't seen him look this awkward since that night when he dumped a soda down her back. If only she could touch his hand, that apologetic little-boy face.

"So," he said, "do you want to tell me what this is all about?"

She couldn't stand to look at the chickens. So she had to look at him. "I—I was angry with your mother." Fresh resentment boiled inside. "She acted as if my children were dirty little animals."

He grimaced. "I can understand that. Unfortunately, Mom had one of her bad days."

Bad days, as in sick? Or hormonal and hot-flashy? Or bad days as in off-the-charts mean? Lauren sighed. "Ethan didn't help matters. But at your house, your mother disliked us from the get-go. When we first met her, she seemed cordial enough. Why the change?"

Now Kyle's glance flitted to the chickens. The antagonism in her stomach freeze-dried into a large lump. "She doesn't want you involved with a woman with children, is that it?"

Lauren crossed her arms. "Does she think I'm divorced? Or that I've never been married?"

"No, she knows you're widowed." He dropped his head then raised it again. "She and Dad both would prefer I marry a woman from around here. And yes, someone without kids. Someone they've known since forever."

"Prefer?" She tried to stop the words, but they spewed out. "The way she acted, it's an order."

"Order?" Kyle seemed to fill the walk-in. "You think my parents give me orders?"

She almost stepped back, but stood her ground. "Maybe 'blackmail' describes it better. If you make dating choices independent of your mother's, she will make the woman you care for—and you—miserable."

His eyes sparked. "Isn't that a lot to assume after only one meeting?"

"Trust me, I know what I'm talking about."

Kyle sighed. "You're probably right. Believe it or not, my mother is a loving, caring person—if she gets her own way."

"That I believe."

"But I don't think we're talking about the main issue here. At least, I hope not." Kyle placed his hands on her shoulders.

She fought a shiver of delight. *Please don't touch me. It just makes this harder.*

Instead of letting go, his fingers gripped her. "If after prayer and thought and time, we both believed we should marry, we wouldn't let my mom or anyone else stop us. Would we?"

Now she wanted to look at the chickens. But he was way too tall, his big, muscular body too close... .

"Would we, Lauren?"

She took a deep breath and looked him in the eye. "No. We wouldn't."

"Then what on Sunday changed your mind?" He tried to smile. "It wasn't my cooking, was it?"

She half laughed, half sobbed. "No, no, it was wonderful." *You were wonderful. You were everything I'd ever dreamed of.*

"Then what?"

She wanted to run away. She wanted to throw herself into those strong arms and never let him go.

"What, Lauren?"

How could his deep guy-voice sound like his mother's? Her hackles rose. "When you were juggling—"

"Juggling?" His hands dropped. He stared. "You don't like my *juggling*?"

"I like your juggling. I don't like swords. Or fire. Or—or chain saws."

"Chain saws?" He shook his head as if trying to clear it. "What are you talking about? I've seen it done on YouTube— that guy was amazing. But I've never tried it—"

"That's exactly what I mean!" She burst into tears.

He dug his fingers into the back of his neck, a muscle working in his jaw. "You're upset because I *don't* juggle chain saws?"

She wasn't making sense, but did he have to look at her like that? She gulped and sniffled, trying to explain. "No, I'm glad you don't. But you use them to make your statues. And the fact you watch chain saw juggling on YouTube implies you might attempt it someday."

"Lauren, I—"

"You love danger. You love doing crazy things. I saw your face Sunday night. You know you do."

He sighed, as if she'd drained the life from him. "Lauren, every guy enjoys doing something a little daring. It's just the way we are."

An image replayed in her mind for the thousandth time: Brent on a movie set after an explosion scene, his safety suit and face black with soot, laughing at her near-hysteria when she was mistakenly informed he'd been injured.

A second one played: a sheriff taking her to view his broken, lifeless body in a morgue.

"Just the way you are? Well, my sons are not going to be that way." She flung her hair back and stabbed her hips with her hands, tears pouring down her face. "They will not return to circus practice. They will not grow up taking stupid risks and looking for thrills in all the wrong places. Then maybe no one will have to tell their little boys someday their daddy is dead."

Her hand flew to her mouth. She turned and ran out of the walk-in.

Chapter 16

"Mom, why are we going here?"

Lauren felt Ethan's glare from her SUV's backseat as they turned into Maconaquah Park. "It's a gorgeous day. I thought we'd like a change."

He snorted. "I don't want to swing. I don't want to slide. I want to go to circus practice."

Neither boy opened a door after she parked.

"You said I had to stay home to rest." Logan reminded her. "Okay, I rested four whole days. I haven't had to take my inhaler at all. So I can practice. And Kyle said we need to get our costumes this week."

How she'd dreaded this moment. But procrastination wouldn't make it easier. "Let's go sit on that bench and have a little talk."

Their identical male looks reminded her way too much of Kyle's during the walk-in argument.

"*Then* can we go to practice?"

"Let's go to that bench and—sit—down." Already she was

gritting her teeth. Not good. They were gritting theirs, too. But they walked beside her in the absurdly cheerful sunshine and sat, one on either side, in silence. Two squirrels played tag across the playground, flicking their tails as they chased each other.

She took their hands. "Boys, you know I love you—"

"You want us to quit the circus!" Ethan jumped up, his face ablaze with fury. He threw her hand away. "Logan was right. You didn't want us to rest. You want us to quit."

His brother froze Lauren with a look of cold rage. "You said we could be in the circus. Now you're breaking your promise."

"I didn't know it would be so dangerous." Lauren struggled to keep her voice even. "Every week the stunts grow harder and scarier."

Ethan scoffed, "Tumbling isn't scary."

"The roman ladders aren't very high," Logan insisted.

"But one of your juggling stunts uses flaming clubs." She tried to push Kyle's backyard ring-of-fire act from her mind.

"Kyle is teaching us how to be safe." Ethan parroted him as if he were quoting the Bible.

She drew a deep breath. "Kyle is a very good juggler. But sometimes he does dangerous things."

Logan pulled his hand away, too. "He's been nice to us. He teaches us about God."

Ethan nodded vehemently. "And he makes really good strawberry shortcake."

Tears and laughter almost strangled her.

"Don't you like him anymore?" Ethan demanded. "We thought you liked him a lot. But even if you don't, we do."

"He's our friend." Logan continued the assault. "We like juggling with him, but you won't let us. Are you going to make us stop going to Sunday school, too?"

"Of course not!" She'd better clear this up right away. "This isn't about Kyle."

It isn't?

"I—I—" She covered her face. How could she begin to explain? They experienced a rush now as they performed and watched older children take risks. It could so easily escalate into their father's addiction to danger.

"Mom." Logan again. "Are you praying?"

Praying? Not really. In fact, not at all.

His voice shook. "Would you ask Jesus if we should be in the circus?"

She had shared her faith with them. She had taught them to pray.

But she didn't want to pray.

Why not?

"All right." She opened her eyes and touched his intense little face. Ethan stood nearby, head down, hands stuffed in his pockets. "Both of you pray, too."

They squeezed their eyes shut. She closed hers.

Father God—

"Keep your promise."

She hadn't even reached the praise and thanksgiving part she was supposed to include before petitioning Him.

Sometimes answers came quicker than she liked. *But I didn't really promise, Lord—*

"Really?" His gentle, one-word reply captured her.

She struggled like a butterfly in a jar then surrendered. She'd given her children permission to be in the circus, and she shouldn't go back on her word.

Lauren prayed for another minute or two then tapped the twins' elbows. Their eyelids flipped wide open.

"Boys, I will talk to Kyle about juggling flaming clubs. I'm not sure I'm okay with that."

Tiny lamps of hope lit in Ethan's eyes. Logan leaned toward her as if her heartstrings pulled him.

"But I believe Jesus is telling me to keep my promise. You may be in the circus."

Ethan exploded into the double flip he'd just learned.

Logan did somersaults instead, but they were the best she'd seen him do.

Her own heart turned several somersaults as she watched her sons celebrate, but she gave it a stern warning: they could take part in the circus, but more than ever, she determined not to link their future with a man who knew no fear.

Too bad the unicycles practiced in another building now. She'd welcome a dozen chasing her back to the parking lot, never to enter the circus arena again. Logan and Ethan hardly seemed to notice her angst as they pulled her through the back entrance.

Her nose welcomed the familiar, buttery popcorn smell, and as always, she enjoyed the "we're-in-this-together" energy of the performers. A scrum of kindergarten tumblers formed lines and started their act. Their trainers waved at the boys. "You're going to practice with us later, right?"

"Yeah!" the twins chorused.

"I can do a flip now!" Logan yelled. "Ethan taught me!"

At the sight of her son's grin, Lauren rejoiced—and winced. Was she doing the right thing?

Julie spotted her and, with a big smile, gestured for her to sit with her and Maddy. But Kyle's tall figure rose before her, and her pulse thudded in her ears, drowning out everything else.

He was facing away from them. Ethan and Logan dropped her hands and ran to him. She could hurry and hide behind Julie before he saw her. But she'd hidden enough. Lauren took a deep breath and followed the twins to the juggling area.

She caught her breath when they hugged his legs—something they'd only done with Brent. Kyle hugged them, too, then slowly raised his eyes.

She nodded, making her feet take her forward. He pointed the twins toward the box of clubs. They grabbed some and skittered to the other jugglers.

Kyle walked a few steps. She walked a few steps. Could they could hear each other, standing several feet apart like pedestrians at a stoplight? Still, she couldn't move closer.

"I—I've given them permission to be in the circus," she said.

"Are you sure?" Kyle didn't change expression. "Juggling involves teamwork. Ethan can't miss many more practices and still participate. The same holds true with the boys' other events."

She felt like a prodigal mother. "I'm sorry their absence has affected others. I will see they make their practices. But I don't want Ethan taking part in juggling with fire."

"Okay." He nodded then gestured to a juggler, taking him aside to offer tips on his timing. She'd been dismissed. In front of most of Peru.

What had she expected, hugs and kisses? After all, she'd run out on him at the Sunnyside only days before. Lauren wanted to flee to the library, her car, the church—anywhere but here. But Julie was waving at her again. So were several other circus moms. Lauren trudged to the bleachers, promising herself a quick conversation and an escape somewhere until practice was over.

No matter where he stood to coach, Lauren filled his vision. Even when he thought he'd turned his back on her, his eyes found her as she walked toward the exit. Her long-legged, graceful gait reminded him of a doe who visited his backyard almost every evening. Her eyes did, too.

Stop it, Hammond. She doesn't want you, so give it up. He forced himself to concentrate on the kids' movements, critique their weak points, high-five their accomplishments. Ethan hadn't lost the smoothness that characterized his moves. He probably had continued practice on the sly. Seeing the set of his square little jaw as he juggled, Kyle doubted very much if Lauren could permanently insulate him in the safe, sterile cocoon she envisioned. He glanced at Logan, who'd actually improved. Outwardly, the more submissive twin; inwardly, even less compliant than Ethan. He smiled sadly. He'd fallen in love with her kids, too, but they were not his responsibility, except as their Sunday school teacher—if Lauren allowed that.

Breathing a prayer here and there, he made it through the practice. He even gave Lauren a small smile before she grabbed the twins' hands and marched them outside.

Later he sat on his deck watching the sunset. A short time ago, he and Lauren were walking hand in hand through his woods with the kids, and he was trying to think of a way to talk her into marrying him. Now he could hardly talk to her, period.

He'd tried to resolve their differences, only to discover she still grieved for her dead husband—and that he and Lauren were not only not on the same page but possibly living in different books.

Lord, I thought she was the one You chose for me. But if she is, You'll have to tell her.

A rustle among the leaves near the fence caught his attention. The doe's big dark eyes contemplated his as if he were the visitor and she the owner. She turned and, without warning, bounded away into the night shadows.

Chapter 17

"I like this costume." Flexing his arm muscles, Ethan surveyed himself in Lauren's bedroom mirror. Logan tried to outdo him, while the Labs nosed their way into the picture.

Lauren continued changing sheets, but she kept a keen eye on the Labs. Dogs who chewed slippers and underwear would not hesitate to shred unfamiliar, interesting-looking clothing.

"Don't even think about it," she told them. Twinkie and Dinky regarded her with such innocence that Lauren knew she was right. She turned to the boys to warn them about shutting their costumes in their closet after trying them on. Watching them preen, she had to grin. Logan and Ethan looked cute in their tumbling costumes—bright turquoise spandex shorts and tank tops. But Lauren knew better than to tell them *that*.

"Do we look like real circus guys?" Logan tried to bend his skinny torso into a classic bodybuilder pose.

She coughed to hide her laughter, but part of her didn't smile. *Lord, I don't want them to be real circus guys.*

Logan didn't realize how often he painted her into a corner.

But his hopeful eyes reminded her that although bright, he was just a little boy. A little boy who needed his mom's vote. "Yes," she said, "you look like real circus guys."

"Tanner already has the costume we'll wear for the roman ladder. It's purple, with all this glittery gold on it." Ethan aimed his index finger at his open mouth in a gagging gesture. "We'll look like girls!"

"But Dad wore that stuff in his shows, and he looked cool," Logan reminded him. "And he wore it in some of the movies he did. Don't you remember that Arabian one when he rode all those horses?"

Her heart contracted. Yes, Brent had worn more glitter and sequins than she'd ever donned. She just wasn't the flashy type. "But you're wearing regular pants when you juggle, right?"

Ethan brightened. "Yeah, with a plain old shirt."

"And a *tie*." Logan's eyes glinted. "A tie chokes you. That's worse than the glittery stuff."

"Is not."

Tuning out their debate, Lauren's mind wandered as she spread her quilt and plumped the shams. Kyle, who occasionally wore a tie on Sunday morning, looked great in one. And with his muscles, wouldn't he look awesome in a bright, spandex circus costume?

Stop it, Lauren. She yanked the portraits of him from the walls of her mind, fighting back the tears that threatened. "Enough," she told herself as much as to the twins. She crossed her arms and resumed mother mode. "Go change your clothes. Remember, put them in the closet and shut the door. Then take these dogs outside. It's beautiful weather, and they need a good run."

"Okay, Mom." Ethan, without warning, turned a flip, knowing perfectly well flips made Twinkie crazy. She nearly knocked him down, barking as if a burglar army had invaded the house.

"Twinkie! Ethan!"

Logan turned a flip, too, and for a few moments of kid and canine chaos, the lonely unceasing echoes in her heart and mind went unheard.

Circus magic. Kyle watched it happen every year as boys and girls grew more and more confident.

Twenty feet above him, middle-school girls eased into simultaneous poses on the trapezes, balancing precariously on the bars. They raised graceful arms and hands, releasing the cables, held onto the trapezes only by strength and skill. The work of weeks—actually, years—for all.

He gave them a double thumbs-up. Megan, the chubby one on the end, glowed with shy pride.

Kyle had just finished working with the Ladies of the Silver Strand, the most advanced high wire act of the circus. For the first time, they managed the seven-girl pyramid—a stunt that took his performers to the Monte Carlo Youth Circus in Europe one year. This group might be that good, too. No one hit the net today during the nearly impossible act.

Across the arena, a boy waved at him from one of the roman ladders. Ethan Pellegrino. That kid had never lacked confidence, even the first time he walked into the arena. His smile, so like Lauren's, both warmed and broke Kyle's heart. That Lauren allowed the twins to participate meant a lot to him, but every time he saw them was a reminder he had lost her.

Longing surged through him—if only he could gaze into her eyes again. Touch her and know she wanted to touch him, too. How long would the pain last? With Brittany, the breakup bummed him for a few weeks, but he recovered pretty fast. This ache only grew... .

Ethan, poised near the top, was paying less attention to what he should be doing and more to the kid below him, even jostling the boy. Like many talented kids, Ethan got a little cocky at this stage. He also knew when to time his misbehavior, as the spotters were busy helping the girls do their poses. Kyle quickened his steps to the pair of ladders, only to watch Ethan slip from his position, grabbing uselessly at the ladder as he hurtled to the floor.

"Lauren, you need to go to the emergency room." Julie's voice. But it didn't sound like her.

"What's wrong?" Lauren's fingers froze around her cell. Purdue's course list on the library computer monitor faded into nothingness. "Are the boys okay?"

"Ethan fell."

"Fell?" How could he fall while juggling?

"He fell off a ladder. He seems alert, but his shoulder's hurt. Kyle's taking him to the emergency room here in town. I'll bring Logan home with me."

Of course. Tonight was roman ladder practice. Why did her brain feel as if it were stuffed with sawdust? "Thanks so much, Julie. I—I'll go right away."

She dashed out of the beautiful old Carnegie library to the parking lot. Her SUV coughed as she paused at the exit then mindlessly turned the wrong way.

What is the matter with me? Because of Logan's asthma, she'd checked on the location of Peru's hospital. But this was Ethan, not Logan. Indestructible Ethan, who'd survived Little League without a scratch. Lauren turned around in an alley, peeling out as she roared back onto the street.

Stupid brain, full of sawdust. Circus sawdust. Why had she let it blow into her life, invade her family? But her mind experienced no difficulty in playing and replaying a loop of Ethan lying on the arena floor, moaning in pain. She pulled into the E.R. parking lot without further loss of time. Charging through the brick building's entrance, she immediately spotted her son in the waiting area. Watching the widescreen

TV, Ethan held an ice bag up to a bright red area on his face. Kyle, beside Ethan, held one on his right shoulder.

"Mom!" He sounded as if she could magically make it all better.

"Oh, Ethan." She dropped beside him and laid her cheek on top of his head, since she couldn't hug him.

"Ms. Pellegrino?" An efficient voice called from the reception area.

"Yes." Lauren didn't want to take her eyes from Ethan's face.

"Would you please fill out these forms so we can treat your son as soon as possible?"

Kyle rose. "I'll get them."

She muttered "Thank you," but clouds of resentment swirled in her mind. *You and your circus. If you hadn't talked me into letting the boys participate, Ethan wouldn't be here.*

But she was the one who had prayed then permitted them to continue. God had allowed this to happen. Just as He had allowed Brent's death. *Why, Lord? Why? I try so hard to do the right thing... .*

A toddler with black pigtails wailed on her weary-looking mother's lap in another corner of the waiting area while other children in the family quarreled. When a teen showed up, wheezing like a bellows, the waiting room's very air felt toxic with anxiety. She couldn't help feeling relieved when Kyle returned with a clipboard. Removing the insurance card from her billfold—*Thank You, God, we have insurance now!*—she forced herself to answer all the questions, her free hand holding Ethan's.

Kyle took the completed clipboard. "I'll return this to the nurse. She says I can't give Ethan anything other than water. But can I bring you coffee?"

At his kindness, her heart burned. The last time he'd served her coffee, she'd sat on his deck, pampered and blissfully unaware of the struggles to come. "N—no, thank you." She still couldn't look him in the eye. Instead she focused on Ethan as Kyle headed for the desk. "How did you get hurt, hon?"

"Daniel was bugging me—"

"The boy who does the roman ladder with you?" He'd mentioned Daniel before, not in a favorable way.

"Yeah. He said he was stronger than Logan, and I pushed him. I lost my balance." His lower lip trembled. "I guess I shouldn't have done that."

"No, you shouldn't have. Did you knock him off, too?" She held her breath. "Was anyone else hurt?"

"No." He lowered his head.

She yearned to simply make him feel better, but her son needed to understand his actions had consequences. "Other children could have fallen, too. And you must have hit the floor hard."

"Yeah." He fidgeted with the ice bags. "But it's my shoulder that really hurts. Do you think I'll get to be in the circus anyway, Mom?"

The *circus*? She didn't want to hear the word. But Ethan didn't need a ranting mother. She had to hold it together until they lived through the immediate crisis. "I don't know."

"She'll know more after you've seen the doctor, Ethan." Kyle had returned.

At the sight of the man's big hand gently rubbing her little boy's blond curls, Lauren almost broke down.

Ethan, looking up at him, nodded. A tear or two flowed down his cheeks, but Lauren could see he'd accepted his coach's words.

They didn't wait long, but it seemed forever. She called Uncle Hort and arranged for him to pick up Logan.

"All right if I call the church's prayer line?" Kyle pulled out his cell.

He was the wrong man for her—but why did he always seem to do the right thing? At least, most of the time. "Thanks. I'd appreciate that."

A gurney burst through the ER doors with an EMT holding an oxygen mask over a gray-haired woman's face. An elderly man stumbled after them, his eyes so glazed the nurse at the desk hurried over and guided him to a chair.

I'm not the only person asking "Why, Lord?" Clasping her son's hand, Lauren prayed for him—and for the old man, his wife, and the other patients and their families at the E.R.

Finally Ethan's name was called.

"I want Kyle to go with us, too." Ethan seemed to have read her reluctant mind.

What could she say? "All right." Still avoiding Kyle's eyes, she helped Ethan down the hall to an examination room, where a nurse took his vital signs.

"You're doing fine, Ethan. I hope we can make you feel better soon."

The doctor, a tired-looking man around fifty, greeted them with a pleasant hello. "So we have a circus injury here?" He reached toward Ethan's shoulder.

"I fell off a roman ladder." Ethan, his face wary, pulled back.

"Doc Anderson knows what he's doing," Kyle promised. "He's treated circus-related injuries throughout the years. He used to clown, too."

Did every doctor, lawyer, and janitor in Peru have a history with the circus? Lauren wanted to leave, to take her son someplace where clowns didn't work in emergency rooms. But Ethan's drawn face helped her restrain herself. She watched the physician gently probe his shoulder.

"Ahhhh!" Ethan pulled away from him. "Mom, it hurts!"

She fought to keep her tears from matching his. "I know, hon, but—"

"May I?" Kneeling before them, Kyle almost forced her gaze to connect with his. He looked so concerned that despite herself, she nodded.

Kyle cupped Ethan's face between his hands. "The doc

wants to fix you up like new. So let him. Look at me while he checks you out and tell me the Bible verses we've been working on, and I'll let you throw five pies at me when you're well."

Ethan gave him a pain-filled smile and nodded.

Kyle glued his eyes on Ethan's. "Okay, Ephesians 6:10 starts with 'Be strong.' "

"Be strong in the Lord"—Ethan winced as Dr. Anderson began the examination again—"and—in his mighty power." The boy gritted his teeth, his eyes full of tears.

"Put on," Kyle prompted him.

"Put on—the full armor—of God."

Lauren's stomach lurched as she watched him hurt. *Be strong. Be strong in the Lord... .*

"So that you can take your stand against the devil's schemes!" Ethan quoted triumphantly. "I did it! I did it!" He gave Kyle a weak grin. "You're going down!"

"Guess I am." Kyle shook his head. The twinkle in his moist eyes squeezed Lauren's heart.

"You did good, Ethan." The doctor washed his hands. "I'll talk to your mom, and then we'll fix your shoulder."

The physician gestured to her. Reluctantly Lauren followed him into the hall.

"Did Ethan break anything?" she asked.

"No, but he dislocated his shoulder. I'll have to pop it back."

She gulped. "Will you put him under?" With all Logan's episodes, she'd thought she'd toughened up, but this was different. The examination alone made the room revolve like a merry-go-round.

"We normally use what's called a conscious sedation—your son will be put under, but not completely." He paused. "You may hold Ethan's hand before and return afterward, but I don't permit moms or any other close relatives to be present during the actual procedure."

"I—I understand." She did, but how could she leave her injured child when he needed her most? Biting her lip, she could hardly see through a fog of tears as they reentered Ethan's exam room.

Dr. Anderson hunkered down before Ethan and shared a kid-friendly explanation of treatment with him, giving her time to collect herself. Ethan interrupted. "Can Mom stay with me while you're fixing my shoulder?"

Clasping Ethan's hand, she tried to lighten her voice as she answered, "No, the doctor says no moms allowed. But I'll stay with you as long as I can, and I'll be here when you awaken."

His little fingers tightened around hers. "Then I want Kyle to stay with me." Ethan's big blue eyes pleaded with his coach. "You'll stay with me, won't you? Promise?"

She turned to Dr. Anderson, refusing to link her gaze with Kyle's again.

"He's stayed before with other circus kids while I worked with them."

The doctor sounded so calm. So controlled. So unlike the wild whirlpool inside her.

"It's up to you, Ms. Pellegrino." A nurse entered, and Dr. Anderson rose and conferred with her in a whisper.

"Please, Mom? Please, Kyle?" Ethan looked too weary to launch his usual "please—please—please—please" assault. But his pleading face conquered her.

She raised her eyes to meet Kyle's. Her throat tightened so she could hardly choke out her thanks and "Yes, Ethan, Kyle can stay with you."

If only he could stay with me, too.

"You doing okay?" Kyle took Ethan's hand.

"Yeah." The boy's eyelids drooped as the sedation continued to take effect. Holding Ethan's hand, Kyle thought how much he'd enjoyed getting to know this kid. Though only eight, Ethan shone with inborn confidence. He said what he thought—at home, at practice, at church—it didn't matter.

Every move Ethan made as he juggled proclaimed that this kid would go places, and woe to anyone who blocked his way.

Right now, however, he looked like a pale-faced little kid who wanted his mama, though he'd heroically sent her to the waiting room with the declaration "I'll be okay, Mom. Kyle promised to stay with me."

Looking at her stricken face as she left, Kyle tried to forget the dislocated shoulder he'd seen before. He told himself this one wouldn't be as bad. But when Doc Anderson yanked and popped Ethan's joint as if it were a chicken's, his own stomach dived to his toes. He had to fight the fog that suddenly filled his head.

"Good boy," the doctor muttered. He washed his hands and turned to Kyle. "Went right back in. But he's going to be really sore. He shouldn't mess with it at all until it heals completely." Dr. Anderson's thin lips flattened into a straight line under his gray mustache. Kyle knew what that meant. He hoped he wasn't the one who would have to break the news to Ethan.

"Hey, my shoulder doesn't hurt as bad." Sitting up in the hospital bed, Ethan wiggled with a ghost of his usual energy. "When can I go back to practice? On Monday?" He scanned Lauren's face.

She closed her eyes then forced herself to open them. "Ethan, you really need to rest your shoulder awhile."

"Mom, you always want me to rest." He rolled his eyes as if the past several hours hadn't happened. "Tuesday, then?"

She heard Kyle, standing behind her, clear his throat. But he'd helped enough. It wasn't his job to tell Ethan this.

Fortunately, Dr. Anderson returned and sat on the bed. "You did great, Ethan. How are you feeling?"

"It still hurts some. But I'm all better." Her little boy stuck his chin out. "When can I go back to practice?"

"You're feeling better because I gave you pain medicine," the doctor explained. "But your shoulder's still injured. Mom's right. It will need a lot of rest so it can heal." He touched the boy's hand, and despite her own pain, Lauren felt for the man. How many times a week did he have to deliver bad news?

"Your shoulder can't stand juggling or tumbling at all. And you shouldn't climb ladders right now, either."

"You mean…you mean…" Ethan's lower lip trembled. Lauren slipped to his side.

"I'm sorry, Ethan, but you'll have to wait until next year to be in the circus."

Up till now, her son had tried to be so big, so brave. But at the news he dreaded most, Ethan broke into a deluge of little-boy tears.

What can I say? What can I do? He hadn't cried like this since his father died, and her tears mingled with his as she awkwardly held him as close as she could.

Kyle continued to hover behind them. She felt his concern as tangibly as if he held a blanket, ready to engulf them in its warm folds. Yes, like Brent, he was a man who loved risk. But when Logan's asthma sent him to the emergency room, Brent rarely accompanied them. Kyle, despite their breakup, had not stirred from Ethan's—or her—side since the moment her son was injured.

A small, cynical thought whispered that Kyle, a circus devotee, was only practicing good PR in order to avoid possible litigation. Hadn't he helped out when other children were injured at the arena?

Which proves what? That Kyle cares about kids.

Fiercely Lauren shoved the disparaging voice aside. *He wouldn't give endless hours to the children at the circus and at church if he didn't care. About Ethan.* She kissed her still-weeping son's head. *About Logan, too—*

And about me.

She knew Kyle cared.

But did she possess the courage to care about him?

Chapter 18

*D*ing-dong.

Who was it this time?

Lauren banished Twinkie and Dinky to the mudroom after a joyous assault on visitors, but they still barked, whined, and scratched the kitchen door, aching to join the party. Rolling her eyes, Lauren headed for the front door. Enough guests, enough casseroles. Between the church and the circus, most of Peru had showed up at their door. The incredible small-town outpouring of concern for Ethan touched her deeply. But they all needed a break. Ethan, who fought sleep at every opportunity, actually asked to take a nap. She wished she could take one, too. A look at Uncle Hort, trying to finish his lunch at two o'clock, told her even his hospitality was wearing thin. Praying the encounter would be brief, she flung the door open.

She stared. And hoped she was hallucinating.

"Hello, Lauren. Where's Ethan?" Her mother-in-law, arms full of teddy bears, pushed past her. "Where's my grandson?"

Uncle Hort, already recognizing her from their Skype sessions, had pasted on his company smile. "Mrs. Pellegrino. What a…pleasant surprise." He rose from the table once more. "Would you like something to drink?"

"No, thank you. I flew out the minute I heard of Ethan's injury…from Liz, of course." She turned a cold smile on Lauren.

She tried not to grimace. Brent's sister, Liz, who rarely called, had phoned the day after Ethan's fall. *I must have been out of it when I told her he was hurt. Of course, she would tell Marian.*

"Where is Ethan? How is he? And where's Logan?"

"Out behind the barn." Uncle Hort thumbed toward the building, visible through the dining room windows. "He goes out to the pasture sometimes to think his thoughts and talk to the cows."

"Cows?" Marian didn't bother to camouflage her disapproval. "Couldn't he be trampled? Why isn't someone with him?"

"Exactly where I was going. I'll tell him you're here." Uncle Hort headed to the back door and took his Purdue cap from its hook. Tipping it to Marian, he disappeared through the mudroom.

Dismay mingling with understanding, Lauren watched him leave. So Uncle Hort wasn't an angel, after all. But then, Marian brought out the devil in everyone.

Especially now that she and Lauren were alone. Marian, her eyes black ice, tapped her Jimmy Choo–clad toe. "I'm waiting to see my grandson."

Lauren planed her tone to hard smoothness. "Ethan's asleep. I'm sure he'll be happy to see you when he wakes up."

Marian's face reddened, but her cell gave Lauren a reprieve. Checking it, Marian stormed out onto the porch while Lauren dropped into Uncle Hort's recliner.

She hoped she might die or at least lose consciousness while Marian took her call, but stray phrases from the loud conversation proved too interesting. Marian was talking to

Preston. "No more money!"… "If you think for one minute!"… "Don't come back!"

Lauren also hoped Marian had expended too much energy
in travel and vindictiveness to attack her. However, upon return, the woman didn't miss a beat.

"Liz said he fell while performing in a *circus*?" Marian
invited herself to sit on Uncle Hort's sofa. "I thought you, of
all people, would know better than to allow that."

Tiny cracks of guilt eroded Lauren's fragile resolve to remain civilized. "It's an amateur youth circus. The children
of Peru have been performing in it for forty years, and the
townspeople help them."

"Obviously, they don't know what they're doing."

Now molten anger oozed through the cracks. "Yes, they
do. Many of the trainers performed in the circus as children."
Pictures of Kyle coaching the boys ran through her mind like
a PowerPoint. The image of Kyle's gentle hand patting Ethan's
drooping head in the E.R. lingered. "I've watched them work.
I can't imagine anyone caring more about the kids' safety."

What was she thinking—*her,* defend the circus? Right
now, Lauren couldn't stand the thought of Logan returning
to practice next week.

Marian snapped, "I don't care if they're Andy Griffith
and Aunt Bee in leotards. They have no business doing this.
And you had no business exposing my grandchildren to such
danger—"

"Hi, Grandmamma!" Logan burst through the front door,
Uncle Hort and the dogs following him.

"Logan!" She jumped from the sofa and threw her arms
around him.

Only grandsons could morph an iron-jawed shrew into a
soft storybook grandmother. Watching them embrace, Lauren felt the familiar bite of guilt. She had taken the boys away
from someone they loved very much.

"When did you get here?" A tired but joyous little voice

called from the top of the stairs. Ethan, looking weak but happy, grabbed the banister.

"Remember, don't slide down!" Lauren dashed up the stairs.

"Mom, I'm not dumb." Ethan turned his eyes on Marian, who, though she huffed and puffed, followed Lauren in record time. Logan charged after them.

"Remember his shoulder." Lauren, turning to face Marian, held her arm between them.

"I'm not dumb either." Her mother-in-law glared at her.

Lauren dropped her arm. Marian cupped Ethan's face in her hands and kissed him several times—something he hated. But his shining eyes told Lauren he would endure even that to be near his grandmother again.

"Grandmamma's going to stay with us tonight!" Logan pushed under her arm. "She'll play Legos with us!"

"And make us robot pancakes tomorrow!"

"I would *love* that." Marian sent a grandmotherly smile toward Uncle Hort, watching the scenario from the foot of the stairs.

His expression as pleasant as ever, he sent Lauren an SOS gaze: *What do you want me to say?*

What could he say? What could she do? The boys clung to Marian as if they never would let her go. Almost biting her lip in two, Lauren gave a small nod.

Uncle Hort said, "We're a little crowded right now, but if you'd like to stay the night, we'd be glad to have you."

Marian pounced on the invitation like a cat on a mouse. "Well, isn't that hospitable of you. I'll help in any way I can."

Trying to avoid Marian's triumphant glance, Lauren looked down at her hands. Pain hit her forehead like a sharp stone, setting off endless circles of throbbing dismay. *I'm sure you will.*

Kyle looked for Lauren after church, as always. These days, he felt like a spy, keeping his glances furtive as he scanned aisles full of smiling people. Ah—there she was, wearing the yellow dress she'd worn that amazing night. The first time he'd held her small, soft hand in his. Kyle sighed and gathered his Sunday school materials from the pew. He'd awakened with sore muscles the day after he'd taken Ethan to the emergency room. Was it because he'd fought three hours straight to keep from throwing his arms around her?

He headed to the side exit, continuing his surveillance. Ethan's bruise looked like someone had smashed an avocado on his face. He appeared stiff and tired, but not in pain. A grin tugged at Kyle's mouth. Ethan would probably bask in the attention he'd receive from the kids in Sunday school.

He ventured closer. Lauren looked as weary as she had in the E.R. Who was that dark-haired older lady with her and the twins? He hoped she was a relative who had come to help Lauren.

Kyle hurried down the stairs to the education wing, organized his materials and snacks, and reviewed the main points of his lesson before the gang converged on his classroom. He knocked knuckles with the boys, trying to keep his thoughts where they should be instead of anticipating Lauren's arrival with her sons—when he could enjoy the brief privilege of greeting her outright, looking her full in the face. Now seeing her round the corner with the twins, he gave them all his best smile.

"Hey, Kyle." The twins lit up with identical grins.

"How's it going, guys?" How he loved these kids. "Feeling better, Ethan?"

"Not really." Ethan shrugged then winced. "But that's okay. Dr. Anderson said it will take awhile."

"I'm gonna carry his backpack for him until he can do it."

Kyle could see Logan enjoyed this new role. Pulling out a chair for Ethan at the table, Logan warned their friends not to bump his shoulder.

"Definitely his brother's keeper, isn't he?"

Lauren's voice startled him so that he jumped. How long had it been since she had started a conversation with him?

Her hair curved toward her soft cheek and mouth as if it longed to touch them. Dark semicircles smudged the pale skin under her beautiful eyes, but for the first time in weeks, she looked directly into his. He lost himself for a moment before answering. "Uh, yeah. Has Logan ever thought about being a nurse? Or—"

"A doctor." The woman he'd seen with Lauren gave him a tight smile. "Of course, Logan will be a doctor."

"I was going to say that." Kyle was telling the truth, but this woman's forceful eyes made him feel as if he agreed because she wanted him to.

Lauren's soulful look vanished. "Marian, Kyle Hammond is the boys' Sunday school teacher. Kyle, this is Marian Pellegrino, the twins' grandmother from California."

In reading Lauren, he'd messed up big time the past few weeks. Still, he knew without a doubt that as far as Lauren was concerned, Marian spelled trouble. Great. Not what this tired mom needed. Kyle couldn't help himself. He had to ask. "Is there anything I can do to help?"

She gave him a small but warm smile then, one that drained the breath from him. "I'd like to touch base with you about something after Sunday school."

He tried to keep the eagerness out of his voice. "I'll be around."

Behind her, Marian's gaze probed then speared him, but he didn't care. He wanted to tell Lauren he would be available the rest of his life. But a for-real conversation after church sounded at least like a start.

After Sunday school, Lauren hurried to the twins' classroom, praying Uncle Hort's class would end late, as usual, so she could talk to Kyle. Bless her sweet uncle, he had corralled Marian and taken her to his class before she realized Lauren had slipped away to her own group. The woman acted as if she were Lauren's parole officer.

Good. Several other parents were already leaving Kyle's room with their boys. All she wanted was a minute to thank him for his help at the E.R. and ask him if they could meet to discuss the circus situation. *And maybe...ours?*

She almost jogged down the hall, a good excuse to take a few deep breaths. And ignore her pounding heart. Kyle was conducting his usual good-bye routine, joking with the boys, bragging about them to their parents—"Hey, Tyler answered three hard questions today!"—and retrieving Sunday school papers that had escaped their owners. At the sight of her, he paused.

"H–hi." She felt as if she were back in high school, hoping to meet a boy outside his study hall.

Kyle waved good-bye to the last departing family and turned to her.

"Are the twins ready to leave?" A chorus of yells from inside the room greeted her question.

"They're duking it out with two other guys in the paper plane finals." Kyle waited, his hand digging into the back of his neck.

Blood rushed to her cheeks. "I wanted to thank you again for helping Ethan. And I wondered...if we could meet to talk about the boys and the circus before the next practice. Tonight or tomorrow night."

"I'm tied up today."

Lauren caught her breath. She'd heard through the Peru grapevine that Jenna Sharp was visiting her grandparents this weekend. Was he going out with her?

"But I could do it tomorrow." He leaned against the door-frame, his muscular arm flexed against the wall.

"Do you think we could meet at the library around eight o'clock?"

"The library?"

"Yes. With Marian here—"

"I understand."

No, he didn't. They couldn't talk at the arena, where a couple hundred pairs of eyes and ears would hear their conversation. She didn't want to eat with Kyle at the Sunnyside or any other restaurant, where their meeting could be construed by others—or him—as a date. Still, how could it seem like anything else, with the intensity of his gaze warming her, even if their "meeting" took place in a library? She cleared her throat. "Hopefully, we can work out the circus situation—"

"*What* circus situation?" Marian's voice behind her froze Lauren midsentence. "There is no situation to work out."

Her heart felt as if an arctic spell had been cast on it. She turned slowly and faced the woman. "Yes, there is. But right now, let's take the boys home." She stuck her head inside the door. "Ethan. Logan. Time to go."

Fortunately the twins had finished their tournament, Ethan winning, as usual. Kyle high-fived them and handed them their Sunday school papers with a quiet good-bye.

Lauren had never before seen Kyle's dark eyes blaze as they did now.

Perhaps it was just as well that Kyle couldn't meet her tonight. The twins had been hugged and kissed excessively and tucked into bed by their doting grandmamma. Lauren met her at the foot of the stairs. "Marian, I think we need to discuss some issues, maybe out on the front porch. It feels almost like summer—would you like some iced tea?"

"No, thank you. Apparently they don't sell my brand in Indiana."

"Water?"

"They don't have that either."

Lauren poured herself a large glass of tea and opened the screen door, pausing to look back at Marian. Her mother-in-law, with a slight shrug and eye roll, followed her.

Such a quiet, beautiful May evening. Lauren inhaled the clover-sweet air, loving the rustling rows of green corn plants across the road and the sun's showy farewell. A shame to spoil it all. She dropped into the porch swing, making room for Marian beside her.

Marian sat in the old red metal Adirondack chair instead. She said nothing.

Lauren sipped iced tea, rolling it around to moisten her mouth. "Marian, I appreciate the interest you take in the twins."

"They're my *only* grandchildren." She didn't look at Lauren. "I love them."

"I know." The little catch in the older woman's voice was making this even harder than Lauren expected. "But I am their mother. And I will make the decisions regarding their activities—including the circus."

With Lauren's words, the sweet grandmamma vanished. "You would even consider allowing the boys to participate after all Ethan's been through?"

In one sentence, she'd raised her volume at least three levels. The black-and-white Holsteins in an adjoining pasture raised their heads, as if to eavesdrop.

"Yes, I will consider it." Lauren lowered her voice. "I've thought of several good reasons why I may let Logan continue this year. And next year, I may let them both—"

"I'm sure they're very good reasons." Her mother-in-law changed her tone, almost purring like a cat. "And that they include that tall, dark, and handsome 'Sunday school teacher' who takes such an interest in the *boys*."

Perhaps it was good she felt so mad she couldn't talk. Finally Lauren said, "Kyle is their Sunday school teacher and circus coach. He's a fine Christian man. But I make decisions based on what is best for my boys—"

"Of course you do," Marian interrupted. "That's why you're so willing to put them in a risky situation with potential for even worse danger. Don't you think I know about the trapezes? And the high wire acts?" She rose, her voice full of venom. "No doubt your Sunday school teacher has made you forget all about Brent—you know, Brent, my only son?— and the stupid, needless way he died." Tears rained from her bloodshot eyes, her mouth working as if she might spit on Lauren. "Well, I haven't forgotten."

Beyond anger. Lauren had heard the expression, but she'd never felt it. Until now. Did Marian somehow blame her for Brent's death?

"Let my grandsons perform in this circus, permit them to take up increasingly foolish, unsafe pastimes, and you open the door to more risks, more pain, more loss."

Lauren shrank back into the swing as Marian hovered like a bird of prey. The woman, wild-eyed and trembling, bit each word in two. "Do you want to lose the boys, too? Do you?"

She suddenly turned on her heel and charged into the house, letting the screen door slam several times behind her.

Watching her manic exit, Lauren couldn't help but recall slamming the Sunnyside's walk-in door, spouting words at Kyle that sounded far too similar to Marian's.

Chapter 19

Lauren approached his table in the near-empty adult section of the library. She looked as if she'd tried to dress for the role of librarian: brown skirt, brown T-shirt, plain sandals. No earrings. But Lauren's super-simple style only made her sleek blond beauty stand out.

She was looking at him.

At him.

He tried to keep his smile simple, too—one he would give any good friend. It wasn't working.

"Hi, Kyle." She sat in the chunky, wooden chair beside him and lowered her voice. "I waited until Uncle Hort and Marian returned from going out to eat." A faint grin. "I hope you haven't been here long."

"Oh, no, just hanging out." He'd never tell her he'd arrived an hour ago, mentally rehearsing lines that miraculously would persuade her to let Logan finish the circus season. That would make her listen to his suggestion for Ethan. That would make her fall for him again.

"I love these old Carnegie libraries, don't you?" Her fingers drummed the table in hesitant rhythm. "Marble stairway and panels, with stained glass over the entrance."

"It is a neat old place."

If they didn't move past the chitchat soon, he'd burst.

She paused. "I wanted to tell you that Logan can continue with the circus."

He blinked. No arguments needed? "Uh, great." He fumbled with his words. "Logan was next in line to juggle. Is—is it all right if he takes Ethan's place?"

"Logan will love that." Her mouth curved into the peach-slice smile. "And Ethan will love coaching him."

"About Ethan…" His suggestion wasn't radical, but after the past miserable weeks, he didn't want to detonate new conflicts.

"Yes?" She cocked her pretty head.

Lauren never made anything easy. "Would Ethan like to be a clown this year? No major physical skits, of course—"

"That's a wonderful idea!" Her face lit up, and his inner fireworks exploded.

"He's a natural performer," Kyle said. Wow, he'd achieved two goals within two minutes. Was the library magic? If they stayed here in this spot, at this table, maybe he could achieve the third impossible goal: to make her fall for him again.

He brushed the stupid thought aside, discussing matters such as intensified juggling practices for Logan, help from Hort, and a costume for Ethan.

Their conversation dwindled. He knew he should end it while things felt so positive. But he couldn't pull himself away.

"Kyle?"

"Yes?" Inside he felt the finger of impending doom.

"I want to apologize for the way I've been acting."

At this point, he expected angels to appear. Maybe they'd tell him what to say. "Um—"

"Perhaps I should explain why I'm rethinking some things."

Yes, he would like that. Maybe.

She sighed. "I had a big blowup with my mother-in-law last night."

"Things seemed a little…tense yesterday when you picked up the boys."

"A little?" She snorted. "Marian has never liked me. I wasn't good enough for her wonderful son. Although I did produce two perfect grandchildren."

He liked the little toss of her head. "I suppose she doesn't want those two perfect grandchildren in the circus."

"You suppose right." Her small defiance melted into thoughtfulness. "When I listened to her rant and rave last night about possibly losing the boys, too, I realized she still hasn't coped with Brent's death. And neither have I."

He really didn't want to hear about Brent. Where was a librarian's *"Shhh!"* when you needed one? But he knew Lauren needed to talk about her dead husband. And he needed to listen.

"Although we struggled in our marriage, his death blew me away." Her head bowed. "Actually, it made our loss—the boys' and mine—worse. When I prayed and thought it through last night, I realized I hadn't forgiven Brent for taking unnecessary chances. For his irresponsible behavior." She raised her chin, her eyes teary, yet direct. "So I made that decision. I asked God to help me forgive him."

He didn't dare move. She seemed as fragile as the library's stained glass. But God was at work.

She shook her head. "I should have talked about Brent with someone. But I didn't."

He didn't want to push, yet he so wanted her to heal. "Our church has a grief group, Lauren. You might want to check it out."

"I think I'll do that. For the boys. For my sake. Maybe…for ours?" She raised her eyes, so full of yearning that his heart flew higher than any club he'd ever thrown.

"Yeah," he answered. "For ours, too." One of her oval pale-pink nails grazed his square one. He clasped her hand. Tightly.

She left a short time later.

Her smile permanently imprinted on him, he sat in silence, thanking God with all his heart.

He also hoped Lauren's mother-in-law might still be around at church next Sunday. He wanted to walk up to Marian and shake her hand.

"I did it!" Logan danced around ring three of the arena, waving three clubs like signal flags. "I juggled three for a whole minute!"

"Yesss!" Ethan, cavorting awkwardly, knocked knuckles with his brother.

Sitting in the bleachers, Lauren wanted to throw kisses, but she contented herself with holding both thumbs up. Uncle Hort pumped his fist.

Julie, sitting nearby, waved, too. "Your boys are something."

"They sure are." Uncle Hort wolfed down his popcorn. " 'Course, boys are going to compete. But when the chips are down, those two stick up for each other. I don't have to help Logan much with his juggling. They've been working out behind my barn when they're not at practice." He stood. "Well, better head home and clean up. Marian and I are going with the church seniors to a concert at Wabash tonight. See you later." He gave Lauren a hug and left.

Julie's keen eyes followed him. "Hort and your mother-in-law get along very well."

"I think he entertains Marian mostly to keep us apart. And to distract her from the fact the boys are practicing for the circus."

Logan made another great catch. Kyle demonstrated an even more intricate move for him. How she loved watching him work with the kids. And under the guise of devoted circus mom, she could admire Kyle without the restraint they both practiced when he joined her at the Sunnyside for coffee or an occasional lunch together. Here, she could watch him for hours, and no one would notice.

"Stop drooling, Lauren."

Well, no one but Julie. "Excuse me? I'm watching my sons."

Julie snorted. "And their instructor. And why not? He's sensational. You're sensational. You two should be married by now."

The arena's temperature shot up ten degrees. "I've got two boys to think of. Kyle and I are taking it slowly—"

"Too slowly, in my opinion. Complicates things."

"You and Sylvia." Lauren shook her head. To distract her friend, she said, "I hope you haven't had this kind of conversation with Uncle Hort."

"Nope. Hort's sweet and wonderful. Marian's not."

"You've only heard my side of things."

"Oh, I've talked to her when he's taken her around town." Julie rolled her eyes. "She can hardly take her eyes off him. But he seems to be having fun."

"They're only friends." Lauren folded and refolded her empty sandwich paper. "I appreciate his keeping her busy, but I wish he'd back off a little. Then she'd get mad and go home."

"Sometimes Hort's too nice." Julie made a face.

"Yes, he is." Lauren steered the conversation to how much Ethan enjoyed clown practices. They chatted and laughed and watched elementary-age boys and girls chase after broad-shouldered teens riding balance bikes around a ring. The younger kids shinnied up the riders, stretching into gymnastic poses on the front and back. One girl wearing bright pink leotards pressed her body into a perfect handstand.

Lauren loved watching the children perform. Other children. Her children.

Also—she had to admit it—she really, really liked watching a certain juggling instructor. Even if she drooled a little.

* * *

"Hort, you're encouraging the boys." Lightning criss-crossed Marian's stormy eyes as she walked up the front sidewalk carrying a shopping bag.

Lauren, sprawled in the porch swing, sat up straight, every muscle tightening.

"I certainly am." Uncle Hort didn't take his eyes off the red, green, and blue balls he juggled.

Ethan perched beside Lauren and bragged, "Kyle says Uncle Hort's the greatest juggler in the world!"

"I hope someday I can juggle like him and Kyle." Logan stared at the flying balls as if hypnotized.

"Yeah, Kyle uses machetes! And fire." Ethan's eyes widened in little-boy awe.

Lauren wanted to close hers, but she also wanted to watch Marian's volcanic eruption.

When it came to nasty special effects, Marian did not disappoint. Her face turned purple, her eyes glowing like a gargoyle's. "Lauren Pellegrino, you are responsible for this."

In one smooth motion, Uncle Hort caught the balls and tossed them to Logan. "Why don't you try that trick? Take these out back, where you've got plenty of space."

Clutching the balls, Logan and Ethan dashed past their grandmamma and around the corner of the house before she could stop them.

Marian slowly mounted the porch steps, glaring at Hort and Lauren. "Neither of you see it, do you? No, juggling balls isn't a big thing. But we all know the boys won't stop at that." She glared at Hort then thrust her nose almost in Lauren's face. "A man who juggles fire. Machetes. What are you thinking, Lauren?"

"I'm thinking of marrying him." The words leaped from her mouth before she could stop them, but now that they were out, she liked the sound of them. "What I do is my business, Marian. And that goes for parenting, too."

"So a grandparent has no rights? They're *my* son's children, too." Tears of rage spurted across her face. "He's only been gone a year—"

"Almost two." Lauren crossed her arms.

"—and you act as if he never existed. You'll marry this fire-juggling farmer from Indiana and try to keep me from my grandsons. But my lawyers will have something to say about that."

Lauren wanted to sound off like a siren. But she forced herself to lower the volume.

"You're their grandmamma. I won't take them away from you."

"I'm supposed to believe *you*? You moved them half a world away from the only home they ever knew!"

From a life in which you and dear Preston tried to manipulate every move we made.

"I think the boys feel at home here in Peru," ventured Uncle Hort.

Marian turned her fiery gaze from Lauren to him. She hated that he bore Marian's wrath, too, but enjoyed the moment of reprieve.

The flames in Marian's eyes lowered, flickered, and then died. "I thought we were good friends, Hort."

Did her lower lip tremble? At the hurt in the woman's face, Lauren's stomach plunged to her ankles. *Julie was right.* At least, as far as Marian's feelings were concerned.

"We are friends." Uncle Hort rose. "But this is my niece's home. It's obvious you disagree about the way she raises her boys. You are welcome to visit again, but I think it's time you went back to California. I'll drive you to the airport."

"You certainly will *not*." Marian swept past him into the house and up the stairs. In the odd silence, Lauren stared down at her hands.

"Don't blame yourself, Laurie-girl."

She'd been right, but awfully blunt. "Maybe I should apologize—"

"Apologize?" Horror filled his face. "Don't apologize! Then we'll never get rid of her."

Chapter 20

"If you flip that brush at me one more time," Lauren said, "I'm going to dump my whole bucket of paint on your head."

"It was accidental." Summoning his most innocent expression, Kyle paused in painting the arena's green bleachers.

"Right. I have two boys. I know how you guys think. Thank heaven the rules say the twins are too young to help."

She was right, of course. He and his high school buddies had perfected the "accidental" brush flip throughout years of preshow arena preparation. "The circus board won't like it if you waste paint on me."

"Maybe they'll throw me out." Her evil chuckle startled him. "That will leave you to finish all by yourself."

"You wouldn't do that."

"Try me." Her dark eyes glinted.

"Okay, okay." He raised a hand. "I'll behave. I don't want to miss dinner with you."

She smiled, and his heartbeat shifted into high gear.

Dressed in grubbies and a bandanna, Lauren still couldn't look more beautiful.

"You just don't want to miss Hort's chili."

"Well, that either." After supper, when the twins hit the sack, maybe Lauren and he could spend quiet time on the front porch. For the first time in weeks, they'd be alone.

But first he needed to finish these bleachers. He dipped his brush in the bucket, glad so many people from the community had pitched in, as well as friends and relatives of the performers who had already arrived in town for Circus Festival week.

By late afternoon, the circus arena had been washed, painted, and dusted into shining expectancy. The rigging experts, like industrious spiders, had been weaving their magic across the ceiling all day. Kyle helped check safety nets and every inch of high wire his performers would walk. Giant polka-dotted balls lined one wall; trampolines, folded into sections, stood at attention at another. The sideshow characters on the huge, colorful vintage banners looked down from their lofty positions as if to supervise the whole operation. Only a faint popcorn fragrance wafted through the arena because the concessionaires had scrubbed every corner of the wagon to ready it for hungry audiences next week. As far as Kyle could see, the circus was ready. Let the show begin!

While he waited for Lauren to finish cleaning up, he stood inhaling the huge room as he did every year, absorbing its enchantment. If someone handed him a fistful of cash and said, "Kyle, you can go anywhere in the world," he wouldn't budge from Peru, Indiana. Although actual circus sawdust had disappeared down through the years, along with Horace the Horse-man and Serena the Snake Charmer, it had become a part of him.

Lauren rejoined him. "This place is incredible."

"I should get tired of it. But I never do."

"You're just a big circus kid."

He grinned, hesitating a little. "Is that so bad?"

"No." She matched his grin and took his hand. "Maybe it's pretty good."

"I'm not going, and that's all there is to it." Mom slashed open a bag of rabbit pellets and dumped them into her pets' dishes. The rabbits, no doubt delighted at her reckless generosity, still scampered to the opposite end of their cages to avoid her irritation.

Kyle, grooming and feeding the horses, knew exactly how they felt. "You don't have to go to the circus. No one's making you."

Still he couldn't quite believe it. His mother, one of the original high wire walkers from the 1960s, had served on the circus board, along with his dad. Not go to the circus on Family Night? Unthinkable.

"Are you trying to talk Dad out of going?" He scratched Flourish's ears, attempting to keep calm.

"I don't think he wants to." She turned the rabbits' Conway Twitty album up to earsplitting levels.

Kyle raked dirty straw, wishing he could shovel out the stuff between his parents and him as easily. *Lord, what do I do?* The more he connected with Lauren, the surer he felt she was the one for him. Still, if things somehow didn't work out between them, he couldn't and wouldn't cave in to his mom's edicts anymore. Blackmail, Lauren called it. She was right.

He propped his rake against the barn wall, turned down Conway Twitty, and headed for the cows' stalls, where his mother was swabbing udders before attaching them to the milking machines.

Mom wasn't real gentle about it. *Poor cows.* "I need to talk to you."

She didn't stop. "I'm busy."

"You've never been too busy for me."

She straightened. The hand holding the rag dropped to her side. "All right. Talk."

"Talk about what?" Dad, his foot dragging, entered and slapped the rump of another cow, who headed for her stall.

"You're supposed to elevate your leg." She glared at him.

"I've had enough of sitting in the recliner." His weather-beaten face tightened into a straight-lipped mask. "What's this you want to talk about, son?"

Kyle knew Dad's hip was hurting. How had he picked the worst time in the world for this conversation? But he couldn't put it off anymore. He took a deep breath. "Mom, Dad, we've talked about Lauren and her boys before—"

"We've talked about her too much." His mother twisted her rag as if she'd like to wring his neck. And Lauren's.

"I know you're upset that we're dating again, and that's why you're not going to the circus." He softened his voice. "Mom, you went to every single show to watch me when I was a kid. You've come to watch the children I've trained. You love the circus."

She said nothing, but her tired eyes spat sparks at him.

He shot a *"Help!"* prayer up to God, took a deep breath, and placed his hands on her shoulders. "I'd love for you to come. But even if you don't, I'm not going to change my mind about Lauren. I respect you as my parents"—he looked into his dad's face, too—"but if God brings Lauren and me together, I ask that you respect us. If you refuse, I will work elsewhere—"

"You would leave your father alone?" Mom's fists clenched like a prizefighter's, and her nose turned as red as Rudolph's. "You'd do that, with this surgery coming up—"

"Of course I won't leave now. But my long-term plans will change, though I love the farm as much as you do." Sadness welled up in him. "I hope I don't have to. But if you leave me no other choice, I will."

He touched his mother's cheek and his father's shoulder then walked back to the horses' stalls, praying with every step.

"Too bad Kyle and the boys are busy getting ready for the show tonight." Uncle Hort climbed onto the hard metal Tilt-a-Whirl seat beside Lauren and pulled the safety bar past their knees.

"We'll take the kids to the festival after the weekend. But I haven't gone with you on the rides since I was a little girl!" Memories of fun days with Uncle Hort, Aunt Kate, and her cousin Angie crowded Lauren's mind.

Now alternately laughing and screaming as their car spun madly, Lauren hoped she'd hang on to her lunch. When they finally disembarked, the midway continued to rotate around her. *Um, what's my name? Starts with an L...*

Uncle Hort experienced no difficulty stringing sentences together. He joked with half of Peru's population as they strolled past food booths, craft tents, and carnival games.

"Let's stop by the stand before we go to the show," he said. "I want to make sure things are going well."

Lauren's scattered childhood memories returned at the sight of the little white concession stand with its bright blue and gold scrolled sign, Hort's Heavenly Elephant Ears. How many times had she helped him cook at festivals in neighboring counties? Next week, she, Logan, and Ethan all would take a turn. Right now, one of his retired farmer friends manned the booth.

"Sure you don't want an elephant ear?" Uncle Hort grinned.

"I'm sure." Right now, she couldn't even breathe the yummy fragrance. "Maybe after the show."

When they reached the circus arena, he took her arm so they wouldn't lose each other in the crowd. Opening night was Family Night. Only parents and relatives of performers came. After weeks of drop-off and pickup at the back door, they entered, like guests, at the front under the clown sign.

"What a band!" Entering the arena, the "ta-da!" opening strains of the music stirred Lauren's ears as much as the lit-up arena dazzled her eyes. "They're really good."

The trombone section slipped and slid into a wild, fun song. "Hear that? It's called 'Trombone Miss.' " Uncle Hort bobbed his head in rhythm with the music. "Wouldn't be a circus day without that one."

No performers yet, but the air fairly crackled with their energy. *Lord, please help the boys have a good day.* She scanned the arena where she had seen so many children practice so many hours. *Please help all the kids have a good day. And keep them safe, Oh, God.*

She tried to keep her mind off the surprise Logan had planned for Ethan. Thank heaven, Kyle insisted Logan discuss it with her first before he helped with the project. Still—she needed to think about something else.

"I'm surprised so many people make time to play in the band." Lauren scanned the section above the concession wagon, chock full of red-shirted musicians. "They must practice for hours and hours."

Uncle Hort snorted. "That's only part of 'em. I guess more than two hundred take turns—which is good, since the band plays the whole time. Some of them come from out of state to play."

A rainbow-spangled, orange-haired adult clown wearing striped socks zoomed on roller skates through the entrance, scattering spectators. The clown, wiggling her hips to "Hey, Baby," rocketed across the arena, skillfully zipping in and out among black-shirted stage hands, who were checking equipment and hoisting pulleys. Only when the band slowed her rhythm and she threw a big, grinning kiss to the gathering audience did Lauren recognize that face-wide grin under the makeup. Julie!

Lauren hardly had time to wave when a contingent of tiny clowns marched in and began their cute routine: kindergarten-age girls with sweet painted faces, wearing ruffled checkered skirts and huge bows on their heads, and boys dressed in crazy clown suits and big, floppy shoes. One little guy wearing an enormous newsboy cap captured Lauren's heart. "Adorable!"

Although she hadn't figured out the multitude of family connections here, she knew he and many other children were at least third-generation performers.

Lauren glanced at her program. Ethan's age group would clown later. She peered through the binoculars she'd brought and readied her camera settings.

"Lad-eez and gentlemen, boys and girls!" The spotlight went up on a blond ringmaster, resplendent in sparkly red and black. She announced in a professional, mellow voice, "You are about to witness the greatest show on earth: *our* circus, put on in *our* town by *our* children!"

A roar of applause greeted her words. Uncle Hort and Lauren stood, along with all the other family members who had carted their kids to practice and spent hours sitting on the bleachers, eating fast-food meals and helping with homework while siblings practiced their acts.

"Congratulations, Laurie-girl. You're a circus survivor." Uncle Hort gave her a hug and two thumbs up.

"So far, anyway." She tried not to think about Ethan's injury. And Logan's secret. Still, this at-home sense of community felt good.

As they dropped into their seats, the three circus rings lit up. Though Lauren had seen many acts during practice, the young performers' skill and poise took her breath away. Elementary-age girls walked, somersaulted, and flipped off a balance beam called the russian bar, which was held several feet above the ground by boys in embroidered vests. Other children fearlessly jumped off ladders onto teeter-totters, flipping pint-size acrobats onto the shoulders of their larger friends. Twelve- and thirteen-year-olds in glittery pink costumes dangled from white ladders that swung from the ceiling above the audience, balancing their bodies and feathery headdresses with superior skill. In the next round of performances, the unicycles dominated ring one, zooming in complex patterns and linking arms to earn the applause they deserved. In the center ring, younger children showed off strength and flexibility as they did stunts on the rings. In ring three, thirty-plus boys and girls climbed and posed on the roman ladders. Lauren trained her binoculars on Logan. Ignoring his despised purple sequined outfit, Logan stretched his skinny muscles as he spanned two ladders in his pose.

"Quite a boy you got there." Uncle Hort gave Lauren a gentle nudge.

Pride and gratitude welled up in her. Logan had come a long way since they'd arrived in Indiana. When had he suffered his last asthma attack? She couldn't remember. If only her sons would stay away from the more dangerous stunts.

A tribe of elementary-age clowns pranced in Ethan brought up the rear, dressed like a miniature Emmett Kelly. To her surprise, nothing disguised his sling. The corners of his painted mouth turned down. Dragging in listlessly, he watched the others cavort in front of the bleachers. Two of them pantomimed laughing at him. Surely this had to be part of the act. Still, Lauren couldn't help the righteous wrath that surged through her veins.

"Down, Mother," Uncle Hort whispered. "Watch."

The tormentors turned away, absorbed in conversation. An ear-to-ear wicked grin crossed Ethan's face. He pulled a peashooter from his clown suit, pocketing it quickly after he blew it at them. Puzzled, they felt their necks and turned to glare at him. Ethan pasted on his sad face. They turned away again to talk. Lightning fast, he pantomimed kicking their behinds. Outraged, they accused him of subterfuge, only to face Ethan's pitiful gesture toward his arm and a sad, guiltless expression that would have deceived even the most experienced school principal. The audience laughed and cheered as Ethan continued his "innocent" act—even more when, as they did their crazy dance routine, Ethan's athletic one-armed moves upstaged the other children's.

What a ham! Uncle Hort slapped his knee. Lauren shook her head, chuckling. Leave it to Ethan to turn an injury into an advantage.

As the young clowns ran for the exit, spotlights found the Ladies of the Silver Strand high wire act ready to perform, far above the crowd.

"Good thing they had Ethan and the funny stuff before this," Uncle Hort said. "The girls use a net, but this act always gets a bit tense."

The people took a simultaneous deep breath and clung to it as the silver-suited teens performed their seven-girl pyramid. Two pairs of girls standing on the wire held two thin bars perfectly level, while two more girls scaled them and stood on the bars, also holding a thin bar between them. A seventh girl climbed up to it, balancing her body with perfect precision. The entire formation slowly, gracefully moved across the high wire.

Please, Lord. Help them make it across. In the dim light, Lauren spotted Kyle as he stood with the other trainers, his head tilted back. She counted the girls' steps with him. He cared so much for these kids.

All girls this year, but she'd seen photos of guys from past acts. Would her boys someday walk the high wire? Although slow, cautious steps weren't exactly Ethan's style.

"Trust me."

Funny. God had said these words to her so many times lately. Well, that was the bottom line, wasn't it? Circus or no circus? At the last grief group meeting. Even afterward, when she'd chatted with another mother of twins—who had just received their drivers' permits.

As the Ladies finished their amazing stunt, Lauren joined in the crash of applause. *Thank You, Lord!*

The lights went up for intermission, and Uncle Hort tramped down the bleachers, headed for the concession wagon. As everyone stood and stretched, several people from church congratulated her on the boys' acts, giggling anew at Ethan's antics. She breathed an empathetic sigh of relief with mothers of russian bar performers, high-flying acrobats, the Ladies of the Silver Strand. Like her, they felt the terror of letting their children go, frustration when they failed, and joy when they succeeded.

Embraced again with a sense of belonging, she almost missed Kyle's parents sitting on the opposite set of bleachers. Instantly she felt as if she had been beamed outside the city limits. His parents sat like large cardboard cutouts, eyes fixed on her. Too late to act as if she didn't see them.

Lord, I'm tired of apologizing for my existence. Please help me.

Lauren straightened her shoulders. She lifted her chin, coaxed a smile onto her face, and raised her hand to greet them.

To her utter amazement, Mr. Hammond raised his. After hesitation, Mrs. Hammond raised hers. Their movements resembled those of robots. But they had acknowledged her.

The smile she sent across the arena didn't have to be coaxed. And the satisfying sense of belonging trickled back as Uncle Hort returned and the lights went down for the second half of the show.

Dozens of eager beginning tumblers proved a crowd favorite. Crouching in orderly lines alone the mats, they waited then somersaulted, cartwheeled, and flipped. Lauren winced as Logan's double somersault wandered a little sideways, but he'd improved. Multiple trapeze acts dazzled the spectators. Teen girls, hanging far above the audience by their teeth, spun in the air like skaters with no ice.

The jugglers leaped into the center ring, most of them

tossing clubs with the casual skill of experts. Lauren's heart contracted at the sight of Logan, by far the smallest. Face wrinkled in concentration, he could not match the ease of more experienced performers. Still, he held his own, smoothly juggling three clubs and even tossing up a few flourishes—dropping them only twice. He slipped back into the darkness when the others ran their complex routines; smaller jugglers mounted the shoulders of the larger performers without breaking their rhythm, parading around the ring. She gripped her bleacher seat when Kyle, in semidarkness, lit his jugglers' clubs. She knew Logan would not participate in their fiery triangle, yet the familiar tornado of fear whirled inside her.

Uncle Hort's gnarled fingers pressed hers. "It'll be all right, Laurie-girl. You'll see."

She didn't want to see. But as he held her hand, she forced her eyes open. Three young jugglers, like powerful wizards, wielded their clubs with pinpoint precision. Even she had to acknowledge the blazing beauty of their patterns. When one club flew to the side, obviously out of sync, Kyle tossed it back, and the boys compensated for the mistake—how did they do that?—without interruption. At the end, the audience gave a universal murmur of admiration before they applauded.

"See? I knew you could handle it." Uncle Hort squeezed her hand. But he didn't release it because he knew. He knew the hardest was yet to come.

"Ladies and gentlemen!" The ringmaster's voice echoed again throughout the arena as two spotlights went up. One on Ethan, standing at the exit, his painted mouth hanging wide open; one on Logan, standing alone in the center ring, looking hardly old enough to tie his shoes. Lauren's stomach lurched.

"Logan Pellegrino, a first-year juggler, would like to dedicate this special stunt to his brother Ethan, who suffered a fall several weeks ago during practice and was unable to juggle this year."

Kyle knelt beside Logan. She felt his prayers, along with hers.

Kyle lit first one club then a second. A third.

Uncle Hort's strong, sinewy arm encircled her.

Keep your eyes open, Lauren. You can do this. You can do it for the boys.

Slowly, carefully, Logan began to juggle the flaming clubs. One. Two. Three. One. Two. Three.

As he juggled, a spatter of applause, like summer raindrops, shimmered through the crowd, gradually rumbling into a thunderous tribute. Rivulets of tears wet her cheeks.

One. Two. Three. One. Two. Three. He juggled only seconds, but they spanned hours. She fixed binoculars on Logan's face. Straight little mouth. Eyes intense as if the universe depended on the skill of his small hands.

Logan caught the clubs and bowed. Kyle bounded out of the darkness, took the clubs, and gave him a big hug to the background of more applause. Ethan, fast as ever, dashed from the exit and joined them.

Lauren, almost crushed in Uncle Hort's embrace, finally exhaled. *Thank You, Lord. Oh, thank You.*

Kyle felt like Christmas, though the July heat stated otherwise. The strings of colorful lights decorating Hort's little stand and dining tent shone on him, Lauren, the twins, and Hort as they celebrated the best Circus Family Night ever.

Even Kyle couldn't eat another elephant ear, though Hort tried to sneak "just one more" onto his plate. Kyle leaned back in the rickety metal chair, feeling full in a hundred different ways.

Full because Mom and Dad came to the circus. Because his groups had surprised him with their best performances ever. Because he loved Logan's and Ethan's holidayish faces, lit by carnival lights and wonder. They chattered until their get-up-and-go finally went, and Hort took them home.

Best of all, Lauren filled the night. The lights found her hair and eyes, and he could hardly keep from staring at her. She appeared a little weary as they rose to leave, but fatigue couldn't diminish her glow—or the voltage of the look she gave him.

Stunned, he felt surprised to find himself still on his feet. "Want to go to Mississinewa?"

"I thought you'd never ask."

Chapter 21

"Pigs are cool." Ethan tossed corn into his favorites' trough. A dozen squealing piglets made a mad dash for the prize. "They never have to wash up before supper."

"Yeah. I like their tails, too." Logan aimed the cell phone he'd borrowed from Kyle at the twelve little rumps.

Kyle steadied his hand. "What are you going to do with all these pictures you're taking?"

"Just keep them to look at. Or send them to Grandmamma."

Pictures of the pigpen. Marian will love that. Kyle hid a grin. Fortunately, he hadn't given Logan access to his phone when he took the twins for a ride on his combine. Even Marian's past tiff with Hort probably wouldn't keep her in California if she saw her grandsons aboard the lumbering monster. But what she didn't know wouldn't hurt her, and it would definitely help Lauren. And Hort. Kyle gestured with his head. "Come on, guys. Let's go say hi to my dad."

They scrubbed in the mudroom, shedding their "eau de sow" fragrance then headed through the kitchen. Weeks had passed since the circus. Soon the boys would return to school. Just once, it would be nice if his mother stuck around when he brought them to visit. Maybe if Mom had had a hip replacement, too, she would have been forced to remain stationary and get to know the twins. Sighing, he led them to the living room.

"Hello, boys." His dad, seated in his recliner, bumped knuckles with Logan and Ethan, as Kyle had taught him. "You been out running my farm for me?"

The boys went into a long, detailed description of every plant, animal, and machine they'd seen that day. Dad, answering their questions, looked happier than he had at any other time since his surgery.

"Does your leg hurt today?" Logan ran his fingers over Dad's cast. "Are you feeling better?"

The little guy had won Dad's heart with his frequent serious inquiries about his health. "I'm good. Just have to behave and do what the doc and Mrs. Hammond tell me."

"Doesn't sound like much fun." Ethan frowned.

"It isn't." His dad rolled his eyes heavenward.

"You stop that right now, Al Hammond."

They all turned guiltily toward the kitchen. Kyle's mother crossed her arms. "As if I haven't worked my fingers to the bone taking care of you."

Oh, boy. Kyle stood and pulled out his cell. The twins backed behind him. "Guys, maybe we'd better see if your mom's off work yet."

"You're going to send growing boys home without a snack?" Mom sounded as if he'd committed an unpardonable sin.

"Uh, well—"

"I just baked these this morning." She pulled Grandma's puppy-dog cookie jar from the top of the fridge, opened it, and held out two chocolate chip macadamia nut cookies.

Kyle's stomach gave a loud growl. Too long since he'd eaten

Mom's cookies. Ethan and Logan emerged from behind him, their eyes like flashlights.

"May I have one?" Kyle gave her his little-boy look.

"I want one, too." His dad sounded like he'd dropped sixty years.

Her mouth was fighting a losing battle to keep its frown. "Oh, all right." She distributed cookies, chiding his dad— "Only one for you. Remember your cholesterol."

Kyle munched the crunchy, chocolaty treat. Mmm.

Ethan chomped away. "Wow! These are even better than Uncle Hort's oatmeal cookies."

A flush of pink colored Mom's cheeks, but her nose remained nice and pale. Her eyes sparkled.

Kyle read her mind. Though the fair judges last year hadn't made the right choice, Ethan had confirmed what she'd always known: her cookies were the best in Miami County. Better than Hort's. Always. Forever.

She held out Grandma's cookie jar again. "Want another one?"

Kyle sent up a silent prayer of thanksgiving.

For once Ethan had said exactly the right thing.

Lauren parked at the Hammonds', taking care not to block entrances or exits. She wandered to the barn, listening for Kyle and the boys. Near silence. She wandered out into the nearest pasture. Kyle often took the boys to ride here—this spacious patch of uncultivated grass dotted with black-eyed susans, feathery goldenrod, and white Queen Anne's lace. The blue sky arched over her head like a cathedral's ceiling. She wished she wore a long, full skirt instead of khaki shorts so she could twirl in the sunshine like a character in a prairie romance. She peered over a small rise, her hand shading her eyes. Kyle, holding Flourish's bridle, waved to her. But no twins in sight.

She cupped her hands and yelled, "Where are the boys?"

"With my folks!"

Even from here, she could see the grin that stretched across his face.

Had she heard wrong? Kyle might leave them briefly with his dad, but his mother, though civil lately, certainly hadn't rolled out the red carpet for her or the twins.

Now Kyle mounted his horse. He was galloping toward her, faster and wilder than she'd ever seen him ride. Still that unspeakable smile on his face. Faster. Faster.

Her heartbeat galloped with him, instincts screaming for her to run away. Danger! Danger! But her feet didn't budge.

As he approached a hundred feet away—then fifty—then twenty—and Flourish's hooves shook the earth, she saw the untamed gleam in Kyle's eyes.

She didn't want to escape. Ever.

As Flourish pounded past, Kyle's strong arm curled around her waist, lifting her onto the horse in front of him, pulling her so close she could hardly breathe.

They seemed to gallop forever, Kyle guiding the horse through pasture after pasture. Finally Kyle slowed him to a walk. "Whoa, boy." He dismounted and helped her down.

As he took her hand, Lauren finally found her voice. Sort of. "Where—how—"

"A little circus trick I learned when I was a boy."

"So you galloped across Miami County grabbing girls off farms?"

He grinned. "No, actually a buddy and I practiced it until we could pull it off." Kyle's hand cupped her chin and turned her to look at him. "This was completely different. I've never done that with anyone else."

The smile again. His hand pressed her to him.

No escape. She shivered with delight.

"Lauren, I love you."

"Kyle, I—I—" Everything in her wanted to shout her love for him, too. "But the boys—your mother—"

"Ethan told her he liked her cookies even better than Uncle Hort's."

"He did?" She felt a faint glimmer of hopeful surprise, though she prayed her oh-so-truthful son wouldn't blurt this to her uncle.

"Hort's cookies beat Mom's out at the fair last year. I don't think she's ever fully forgiven him." Kyle chuckled then shook his head in amazement. "But Ethan's comment worked some kind of magic. Mom invited the boys to supper tonight. You, too."

Tears streamed down her face. She hiccuped then snuffled, borrowing his handkerchief to blow her nose.

"This isn't very romantic." He sounded disappointed, but his eyes twinkled. "I thought after sweeping you off your feet that you'd melt into my arms like a girl in a movie."

She dropped the hankie, grabbed his collar, and pulled his face down to hers, kissing him so hard she thought her lips would burst.

"Romantic enough for you?" She gasped when they both ran out of breath.

"Don't think so." He kissed her again and clasped her face in both hands. "I think I'll need at least a lifetime of this."

Lauren pulled his gaze into hers. No escape for him either.

The teasing note left his voice. "Make it love for a lifetime, Lauren. Marry me."

"Yes," she whispered. "Oh, yes."

"Can't choose a much better day for a wedding than Valentine's Day." Uncle Hort raised his goblet in a toast to Lauren and Kyle. "A special day for two incredibly special people."

"Yay!" Logan and Ethan, sitting with her and Kyle at the head table, cheered and waved their glasses of red punch. Both Lauren and her new husband reached a hand to calm their sons and save their clothes, smiling at their excitement, smiling at each other. Smiling.

Dozens of guests seated around long, red-covered tables in their church's activity center raised their glasses, too. Lauren rose and threw her arms around her uncle. "Special? I never would have seen this day if you hadn't helped me and the boys when we needed it most."

Even Uncle Hort's ears were turning scarlet. He slid an arm around her. "Laurie-girl, it's going to be hard to get used to quiet again."

She kissed his leathery cheek. "Well, if you need noise, Uncle Hort, you know where to find it. You're welcome at our home anytime."

"Absolutely." Kyle gave the old man a bear hug.

They resumed their seats and feasted on the delicious sandwiches Sylvia had prepared.

"Keep it simple," they'd told her, "like a picnic during Circus Festival time."

In Sylvia's talented hands, even a simple chicken sandwich tasted divine. Lauren chewed slowly, savoring Sylvia's secret herb cream cheese spread that she used instead of mayonnaise. But the recipe, along with many others in Sylvia's culinary repertoire, was no longer secret—at least, not to Lauren. Much to her—and Kyle's—delight, Sylvia had given her an enormous loose-leaf collection of them as a wedding present. Along with a share in ownership of the Sunnyside.

Now Kyle sneaked a quick kiss and took another bite. "Mmmm. My best girl at my side forever, the best sandwich in the world—and I feel at home here." Giving her a teasing look, Kyle reached behind her, and fiddled with the big red, white, yellow, and blue balloon backdrop for their table.

"Stop it," she whispered, grinning. "The boys will see you and pop every last one." But Kyle was right. Although Valentine's Day had shaped their wedding service, the circus-themed reception he'd requested fit them perfectly. Matching balloon bouquets bobbed here and there throughout the big hall. Bright-colored dishes and gold tableware set off the red tablecloths. The long, gaily decorated tables made Lauren think of circus wagons. And the younger guests, especially, were enjoying the vintage popcorn wagon and cotton candy machine, both manned by Julie and her children in full clown regalia—minus roller skates.

Lauren touched the luxuriant bouquet of red roses Kyle had given her, and then stroked the dark red trim on her slim white satin dress. She hadn't a clue what to wear, but the moment she laid eyes on this one, she knew it was right for her.

"You look beautiful." Kyle raised her hand to his lips. His deep-eyed gaze made her wonder if her cheeks matched her roses, but she threw off her "not-in-front-of-the-children" reservations and returned it.

"You really do look pretty, Mom." Her sons added their vote.

She reached to touch Logan's face, and then Ethan's, and then Kyle's. "Am I lucky to have three such good-looking guys, or what?"

Kyle, dressed in a black tuxedo with dark red vest, defined "tall, dark, and handsome." The twins, resplendent in similar red vests and black pants, had managed to stay clean—so far.

"When do we eat cake?" Ethan licked his lips.

"We'll cut it in a few minutes. Try to stay clean, okay? We'll give you the first pieces after we taste it."

Big grins.

"Then you'd better get ready for the show," Kyle said.

"Yesss!" The twins pumped their fists.

Hand in hand, Lauren and Kyle strolled to a round, red-covered table where Kyle's mother fussed with the four-tier wedding cake she'd made for them.

"Mom, you really outdid yourself this time." Kyle gave her a gentle kiss.

"It's the most beautiful cake I've ever seen." Lauren meant it. Somehow, his mother had designed the elegant white merry-go-round with just the right touches of gold and red.

"I—I'm glad you like it." Rose hugged her son then squeezed Lauren's hand.

It wasn't a hug, but it signified one more step. "Thank you," Lauren said. *For the cake. For your son. For trying to change your attitude.*

Rose smiled. For the first time, Lauren saw a resemblance between hers and Kyle's.

"Hurry, Mom. Cut the cake!" Ethan, at her elbow, had waited long enough.

She'd never liked the smashed-cake routine, but maybe the circus atmosphere made her feel playful. Kyle took full advantage, but she knew he didn't expect the big handful of cake she stuffed into his mouth.

His eyes widened. "I never thought you'd do it," he said when he could talk. "What have I gotten myself into?"

"Too late for you." She gave him a cakey kiss, to the cheers of their guests, who hurried to sample Rose's masterpiece.

"Lad-eez and gentlemen." Uncle Hort, who continued his role as emcee, gestured to a small platform at one end of the room. "Please focus your attention on these fearless young men, Logan and Ethan, who will astound you with their skill and daring!"

They astounded even their mother with their polished exchanges and flourishes. Performing the round-and-round trick, they passed in front of each other, "stealing" clubs to the loud applause of their audience.

"They wouldn't let me watch them practice," Lauren said.

"The boys wanted to make it a surprise." Kyle kissed her cheek. "They're special guys, Lauren. Thank you for sharing them with me."

He rose, shed his coat, and joined the boys, the three juggling in a triangle. Then Logan climbed up to Kyle's shoulders, and the three exchanged clubs as if they had done it together all their lives.

Hours and hours of practice. All for this moment. Dabbing her tears, Lauren approached the platform as the guys finished. She hugged all three as their audience clapped and cheered. *Lord, thank You for making us a family.*

Then Lauren picked up three clubs.

"Mom, what are you doing?" Logan's jaw dropped. For once, nothing came out of Ethan's wide-open mouth.

Lauren smiled, faced their guests, and began to juggle. One. Two. Three. One Two. Three.

Kyle, beside her, grinned and juggled.

The twins grabbed their clubs. Standing one on either side of their parents, they joined in.

The longer they juggled, the more Lauren felt God's applause.

And the audience rose in a standing ovation for the *greatest show on earth.*

* * * * *